THE BEAST ON THE BRINK

THE BEAST ON THE BRINK

Betty Levin

Illustrated by Marian Parry

AN AVON CAMELOT BOOK

THE BEAST ON THE BRINK is an original publication of Avon Books.
This work has never before appeared in book form.

AVON BOOKS
A division of
The Hearst Corporation
959 Eighth Avenue
New York, New York 10019

First Camelot Printing, October, 1980

CAMELOT TRADEMARK REG. U.S. PAT. OFF. AND IN
OTHER COUNTRIES, MARCA REGISTRADA, HECHO EN
U.S.A.

Printed in the U.S.A.

For Victoria

The zoology of dreams
is far poorer than the
zoology of the Maker.

Jorge Luis Borges

BETTY LEVIN has been involved with children's literature for quite some time, and has written five books for young readers. She teaches at The Center for the Study of Children's Literature at Simmons College in Boston. She lives in Lincoln, Massachusetts, with her husband, their three children, one cat, three dogs, twelve ducks, and thirty sheep.

MARIAN PARRY is a distinguished artist and highly original children's book illustrator, as well as the author of a number of children's books. Ms. Parry's work has been presented in many exhibitions and is included in the print collection of the Metropolitan Museum of Art in New York.

1 Some people are born lucky. I'm not complaining exactly, because, as I found out, and you will too, there are other ways of being lucky. Still, I think you know the kind of people I mean. They start out clever or beautiful or athletic. They get names like Dawn or Samantha. And whatever they happen to have on always looks so right that the next day everyone else comes to school wearing the same thing.

My name, Lena, rhymes with hyena. Nobody has ever tried to be or look like me. I used to steal candy and gum from little kids, and I never got caught. I skipped school a lot too. I don't take things anymore and I almost never miss a day of school, and now—NOW—they tell me I have a problem.

My parents say the problem is stubbornness. My teachers say it's too many unfocused enthusiasms.

But the guidance counselor, whose name is Mr. Blanc, doesn't tell me what he thinks. He's always putting things between himself and the kid he's counseling: staplers, stacks of forms, pencil boxes. He builds little walls the whole time and speaks very softly, very low key, about how he's not against daydreams, but that you have to be able to tell the difference between reality and fantasy. He says it's wonderful to have a lively imagination, but there are times when it may have to be curbed.

The first time he talked to me it was about the unicorn. "It's a legendary creature," he said. I agreed with him, but he wasn't satisfied. Our science projects were about extinct or endangered species. I did mine on the unicorn. I had a wonderful time reading about it and I did my outline very carefully.

That's when the trouble started. My science teacher, Mr. Harris, tried to be positive, but he doesn't believe there ever was a real unicorn. "Try the narwhale," he suggested, "which is where the unicorn myth may have come from." He showed me a picture of a narwhale. It was huge and fat. It was gross. It had this spirally horn coming out through its upper lip. Besides, I had done all my work on the unicorn.

Well, I won't go into all the wrangling that went on from there, because that's not what this story is about. What it's about, though, did begin in Mr. Blanc's office when finally, after going round for the fourth time, I said "How do you know it didn't really exist if you don't have proof that it didn't?" and Mr. Blanc raised the wall between us with a cactus plant, a tennis ball can, and a

water pistol. I was dying to know what he was doing with a water pistol.

He said he thought I ought to have reasonable assurance that the unicorn existed. So I had to tell him that I knew quite a lot more than most people about animals because I had spent a lot of time at the zoo (where there are lots of little kids with candy and gum) and had friends there who were rare and unreasonable animals. I could tell he wasn't following me very well. I found myself blurting that I would ask my friends about the unicorn, since they knew more about who was endangered than anyone else.

Well, I get carried away sometimes. I had never mentioned my secret visits with the zoo animals before. What they did after closing hours and what I did with them was our own affair, and none of us wanted any interference from outsiders. But I was so tired of Mr. Blanc's ignorance and those words that cover what he really thinks that I blurted out too much, and suddenly there we were, glaring across the cactus spines at each other. And I had gone too far.

The next thing I knew he was groping around his desk for something else (But what can you put on top of a cactus?), and then he wasn't glaring anymore. He was all soft and unconcerned. What kind of friends did I have in mind, he wondered in a mild, offhand way.

"There's a tuatara," I said. I suddenly realized that it was ages since I'd seen Benjamin the tuatara. I had got so involved in school and things that I hadn't even stopped by the reptile house once. "And a slow loris," I continued, thinking of Jerry's great round eyes, his deep fur, and the way he would curl up like a soft warm ball in my pocket.

Mr. Blanc made his lips smile. "More legendary animals?"

"Real!" I exploded. "As real as you or me. Ask ... ask anyone." I hadn't finished telling him about the rest, but he didn't seem to care. Mr. Harris came in and confirmed the fact that a tuatara is a real live miniature dinosaur and that a slow loris is a simple primate. Mr. Harris could see that Mr. Blanc and I were not exactly hitting it off. He wondered if we weren't really making a lot of fuss over nothing and why not compromise to end the deadlock.

By now Mr. Blanc was muttering something about imaginary conversations with animals being as clear a sign of immaturity as dreaming up imaginary creatures. And I was thinking: Never mind all that, but what if someone goes out to the zoo and checks out my friends there; that would put an end to their secret lives. So it seemed best to shut up and compromise. Though I held out against doing my report on the narwhale.

That's how I ended up with the Asiatic two-horned rhinoceros. This was my teacher's attempt to find something for me that would bear some resemblance to the unicorn. It was nice of him to bail me out of the guidance counseling, so I didn't try to explain that as far as I was concerned I had not become attached to the unicorn for its horn. Anyhow, Mr. Harris said I could change my mind if I came across something I preferred, and that I didn't have to hand in the report before our field trip, like the other kids. Since I was starting over, I could have the extra time, just as long as I was ready to talk about my animal on our trip to the Institute for the Study of Endangered Species.

But on the day of the field trip I wasn't ready. I knew that the Asiatic two-horned rhinoceros is dying out because it needs a lot of space that's being used for other things these days, but I just couldn't get awfully excited about it, and I was still kind of searching for something to take the place of the unicorn. I kept hoping that somehow or other it would all fall together for me before I was called on.

Anyhow, we had hours to go before we were to give our presentations. The first thing when we got to the Institute was a talk by our teacher about conduct. In a few minutes, he said, Dr. Hogg, who was in charge of endangered animals, would come and tell us about the work of the Institute. Then an assistant would take us around—

But Mr. Harris couldn't go on, because everyone was whistling or grunting like a pig or reciting this-little-piggy-went-to-market. I began to think I might not have to worry about the Asiatic two-horned rhinoceros after all.

Mr. Harris got red in the face. I couldn't hear what he said. And while all of this was going on, in walked a tall woman with shiny brown hair done up in a big loose knot with a pencil in it. In she walked wearing an old lab coat, so it wasn't her clothes or anything. It wasn't any one thing about her. She just had this presence about her, a commanding presence.

It wasn't only me that felt that way. All the kids who'd been grunting and everything just stared, their mouths hanging open. They stared and I stared and Mr. Harris said something about Dr. Hogg, and right away Dr. Hogg started reading out loud from a book by a man she said went to some island to study a kind of sea cow that had just been discovered. It sounded like a long time ago, and he had seen the sea cow families, with the almost grown young sea cows as well as babies, and how they all

tried to help each other when they were being caught and beaten and cut up. All about how the men who harpooned them cut great slices out of them while they were still alive, and how thirty men had to hold one with ropes tied to the boats.

It wasn't like something you watch on television where you turn away from the screen for a minute. We were all there staring and listening and Dr. Hogg was reading, and then she wasn't reading anymore. She slammed the book shut. She looked straight at us and said that twenty-seven years after the Steller's Sea Cow had been discovered, the entire species was extinct. And there wasn't a sound in that room. That's the way she was.

After that she talked about her work. "We're looking for the way animals pass on survival information to their offspring. That means all kinds of things, from the way they get their food to the way they breed and raise their young. The Institute's job is to learn how to maintain endangered species in captivity, though our hope is that eventually such animals can be released in special preserves. But preserves are expensive—especially for animals that need a lot of space. Even those species that have a long history of captivity may be unable to reproduce, because of their needs for hunting and rearing territory. Cheetahs are like that. Though people have used them for centuries to hunt and to be pets, it's only in recent years that we've discovered that those animals must have space and solitude to breed and rear their cubs."

Mr. Harris asked her whether small animals had the same needs as big ones.

"Oh, yes," she told him. "Even some of the most primitive and tiny animals, like some of the marsupials we're studying here, require definite—"

And up went my hand. I didn't mean it to. It just shot up all by itself, and I could hear my too-loud voice asking: "Aren't platypuses more primitive than marsupials?" And that stopped Dr. Hogg. And Mr. Harris stared at me, and all the kids turned and stared too, and I knew they thought I was showing off. How I wished I could explain about Winifred and Ernest, my two platypus friends at the zoo, who are extremely proud of being the most primitive of all. They would have counted on me to speak up for them.

Dr. Hogg said, "I stand corrected. Of course egg-laying animals are the most primitive."

I could feel everyone looking away from me and trying to pretend I hadn't interrupted that way. I knew that unless I came up with something really spectacular, I'd be finished for days. No one would sit with me at lunch, that was for sure.

So then and there I decided to scrap the Asiatic two-horned rhinoceros for good and invent something terrific instead. I opened my notebook. I thought a minute, then wrote down a title: *An Animal on the Brink.*

Dr. Hogg, back in stride again, was telling the class some of the problems they have at the Institute with animals that don't adjust well to being studied. "For instance, the tree shrews. They get nervous if they're too crowded. Then they eat too much, get fat, and when they're fat they can't breed."

I wanted to ask her how come she didn't just keep them uncrowded, but I knew I'd better not open my

9

mouth again. Then, as if she could read my mind, she backed up to explain that the Institute needed to know how much crowding tree shrews could stand before they stopped acting normal so that there would be information about their basic needs for reproducing.

While she was talking, I began to think about how much more interesting the sea cow story was than animals that are endangered because there's less room for them than there used to be. I wondered if my title would make everyone think of something tragic, like the sea cow. Then I changed it. *The Beast on the Brink* is what I wrote.

It was all I needed. Suddenly I began to see this beast—hiding, cowering, hunted to the brink of extinction. And I began to draw him.

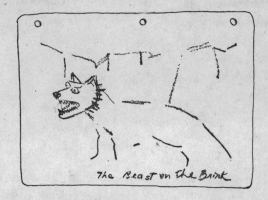

The Beast on the Brink

2 There's something about unnatural darkness and spotlights that give a room new shape. As soon as Dr. Hogg started to show slides and the room was dim and the projector going, my beast took on more definition. It was an animal of dark distant places; it shunned civilization and hid among cliffs and impenetrable chasms, so I knew that its eyes would be special. It had the head of a dog but with the almost yellow eyes of a wolf. Of course I had no color, but I tried to show them as burning embers, pinpricks of fire.

Then we had to pick up our things and be shown around. First Dr. Hogg took us to her lab. I was at the back of the group and didn't get to hear the beginning of what she was telling us. But I saw her showing us this little sort of hedgehog she called a tenrec, and I held out my hands without thinking, the way you do with a small animal, and she put it in them. I knew what the other kids were thinking, but I didn't care anymore because of how Dr. Hogg had answered my hands without ever speaking a word to me.

The tenrec was prickly and cold. It made me feel strange, because it wasn't dead, but it wasn't really alive either. Dr. Hogg said it was estivating, which is like hibernating, only in the summer instead of the winter. Its feet were sharp and dry. Dr. Hogg was worried about it, because it hadn't come out of estivation last year, and now she thought it might be about to, only if it happened too slowly it might starve before it was fully awake because of being so empty and dehydrated. She scowled; she shook her head; but I couldn't tell what she was thinking. She told us that tenrecs are special because they have lots and lots of babies and unique ways of rearing them. She told us they never forget to stop estivating in their natural habitat. She took the tenrec from me and set it down under its heat lamp.

After that she took us into the Observation Room where she had an animal that looked so much like Jerry the slow loris that I was amazed when it turned out to be something called a potto instead. While she talked about the potto, I thought about the way she had scowled over the tenrec and I thought about her voice when she talked about the Steller's sea cow, and I began to imagine how she might sound about my beast.

I opened my notebook and added a few lines to its head and neck. It's almost impossible to draw like that with a notebook half opened, and I made the neck slope away from the head at a funny angle. I didn't want it to end up looking like a hyena, for personal reasons, so I made its body still longer.

I was concentrating so hard on the drawing that I never noticed that Dr. Hogg had gone somewhere else and a new person was showing us other labs and rooms. It was queer, because suddenly I was looking at all these masks they have to measure oxygen consumption on animals with, and the kids were laughing because the animal being measured looked so silly with its mask on. I had no idea whether I would ever see Dr. Hogg again.

At lunch time I ate my sandwich beside the hyrax cage and watched the hyraxes hopping around like pig-

rabbits. All of a sudden it came to me that if I drew one of these animals, people like Mr. Blanc would never believe in it, not unless they'd seen one or a photograph. Hyraxes looked unbelievable; yet they were real. If a hyrax was possible, why not my beast?

So I went back to my picture. I thought if I made the tail good and strong, the back might not matter so much. Only it didn't work out the way I hoped. The tail got too heavy and stiff. It was all out of proportion the way the hind end of a kangaroo is, and the legs ended up looking sort of crouched and catlike. I've never been good at making feet. Usually I draw animals in long grass so that the feet don't have to show. But my background was this rocky cliff, and the feet got bent and looked awful.

I thought about starting over. Then I watched the hyraxes for a while. After that, my beast's ungainly crouching seemed fitting. It had the look of something always hungry, driven into the dark corners of its habitat. No one cared that this ugly beast would vanish from the earth forever.

No one, I thought, except Dr. Hogg. Dr. Hogg and maybe a few other caring people. I could imagine a secret network of them fighting for time. Against all the odds. Just a few people strong enough to withstand the pressures of world progress. And one day I would join them.

Of course I had to picture the moment, years from now, when Dr. Hogg and I would meet again in some remote corner of the earth. Dawning recognition. Wariness. The two of us having given our lives in the service of the rare, the threatened creatures like the sea cow and my own beast. We would come together, Dr.

Hogg and I, in a mighty effort that would give the world a final chance to cherish what it had nearly destroyed.

I thought about my life of service. There would have to be a secret hide-out where a remnant of this species clung to its reproductive life. Some nameless person would be entrusted with its care. Whoever carried that trust, that burden, would live in lonely danger. But I would be equal to it.

Of course that kind of life might be boring too. If a small number of people shared that trust, then you could have vacations and also have company once in a while. Living that way would still be a sacrifice, but it would have more possibilities.

By now lunch was over and we were back in the first room and Dr. Hogg had rejoined us. Kids were reading their reports or trying to say them from notes. Dr. Hogg listened to everyone and sometimes added comments of her own. She sounded interested in everything, even when the reports seemed terribly ordinary. I stared at my beast with its dog-wolf head and enormous jaw, its burning eyes, its cowering look. I wished I was better at feet and tails.

And then I was called on. I didn't even glance up. I knew Dr. Hogg was there looking at me, and I just sailed into my report. Right off, I had to explain about sources I couldn't divulge. Mr. Harris told me to slow down, but I couldn't. I raced through the description of my beast, my notebook half closed so that I was looking at my picture slantwise. I spoke of its great hunger. A wonderful word came to me: voracious. Its jaws, I said, were even stronger than a hyena's, able to crush just about anything to satisfy its voracious appetite.

Mr. Harris said, "Just a minute. Why don't you back up and start like everyone else? The name of the animal and a picture. I gather you gave up on the Asiatic two-horned rhinoceros."

Once I was stopped, I began to stammer. "I made a picture," I said, "a picture from . . . from . . ." I didn't quite dare say: from life. I bent over my notebook, flustered, because suddenly my beast didn't look so very lifelike after all. I pressed down with my pencil and enlarged the beast's teeth. "I'm not that good at drawing," I mumbled. If only I could fix that rear end before Mr. Harris made me show it. I tried to shorten the rump, but I was so tense and the page so unflat that the

line went too far. I tried another line, which only made it worse.

Then, without looking up, I realized someone was standing over me, looking. I leaned over the picture, and all in a rush made more lines so that they looked intentional, like stripes. But before I could finish, a long-fingered hand reached down for the page.

"May I have this?" said Dr. Hogg.

I couldn't find my voice. I nodded.

Striding to the front of the room, Dr. Hogg made her first comment about me. "This student is having a little stage-fright."

I looked up. I could see that Mr. Harris looked extremely doubtful about this, and I couldn't blame him.

"I'd like to help her out," Dr. Hogg went on. Then, without waiting for an answer, she held up my drawing for everyone to look at. "This," she announced, "is an extremely rare animal from Tasmania, an island off

The Beast on the Brink

Australia which harbors many strange and primitive species."

I gasped with wonder and admiration. She really sounded as though she believed in my beast.

"It's a Tasmanian. . . . Tell them," she prompted, her eyes meeting mine with a look of pure frankness.

I gulped, blushed at the sight of those stripes I'd gouged across my poor beast's rear end, and blurted, "Tiger."

My ears were humming; they felt scorched. It was minutes before I could hear clearly enough to realize that Dr. Hogg was carrying on about my beast, not only as though it existed, but as though we were already in clear agreement about its condition.

"While some still refer to it as a Tasmanian tiger," she explained, "others call it Tasmanian or marsupial wolf, since it carries its young in a pouch. Its real name, however, is thylacine. We don't know much about it. It never did well in captivity. No one was especially interested in it until it was nearly wiped out by trappers and sheep raisers. Some people believe it's too late, that thylacine is already extinct. There has been no verified specimen or photograph in over fifty years. But sightings have been reported and probable footprints observed. Finally, about ten years ago, a huge area in southwest Tasmania was set aside as a preserve. It's hoped that if there are survivors, they may begin to breed again. No guns are allowed there, nor dogs or cats because of the danger of distemper, but of course it's impossible to enforce such a regulation. Anyhow, we have no proof that one single Tasmanian tiger or thylacine remains in existence."

Hands waved. Everyone had questions about my beast. Was it like a wolf, or like a tiger? Was it dangerous? How big was it? What did it eat?

And you know what Dr. Hogg sounded like? She sounded like *me*.

I know that's crazy. No one tall with gorgeous hair and a commanding presence and long, capable-looking fingers could in any way resemble me. Yet there was something about the way she laughed and couldn't stop talking, the way she kept interrupting herself, that made me think that any minute now Mr. Harris would begin trying to slow her down.

"Wait a minute," she told us. "Let me see if I can find a photograph. I shouldn't be taking over this report anyway, should I," and she flashed me a smile that was like a signal, and was off, her lab coat swinging, the pencil in her hair flopping precariously.

The way she looked at me! As though she recognized me. As though she was looking at herself. The only trouble was I didn't know how to read that signal. I felt dazed. It had never occurred to me that anyone else, let alone a dedicated scientist, had a mind that actually worked like mine.

It wasn't hard filling in for her, though. And how they listened, my classmates and teacher. I wondered whether I sounded just a bit like Dr. Hogg as I told them, "Fortunately there was one Tasmanian family that cared way back when no one else did. They saved a pair of Tasmanian tigers, which fortunately bred —"

"Fifty years ago?" someone asked. "How long do they live?"

"No one knows," I replied promptly, "because the

Tasmanian tiger never did well in captivity. But some cubs, I mean pups, were successfully raised. See, they grow faster than most marsupials and fall out of the pouch and then—"

And then the door opened. Dr. Hogg carried a big brown volume with one of her long, useful-looking fingers inserted to hold it open at a particular page.

I didn't feel like talking anymore. It looked as though Dr. Hogg liked to live more dangerously than I did. After all, it was one thing to go off looking for a photograph of an animal that didn't exist. It was another to take chances that involved someone else already known for her tendency to be over-enthusiastic and not good at curbing her imagination.

"I have to apologize for this photograph," Dr. Hogg began. "It's not the one I hoped to find."

I let out a long breath. I should have known better than to doubt that woman. She was about to hold up some blurry thing like those so-called photographs of the so-called Loch Ness monster, where somebody has to point out where the neck is and where the tail. Along with all the other kids, I stared up at her; I had no trouble appearing eager and expectant. Dr. Hogg turned the book to us and opened it, swiveling it the way teachers do so that everyone can get a good look.

The kids were leaning forward, because Dr. Hogg had warned us it wasn't the best photograph in the world. I leaned forward too, but I was almost afraid to look.

"The contrast's poor," Dr. Hogg pointed out. She held my drawing up beside the photograph in the book. "Actually you can see how the stripes traverse the rear half of the animal better in Lena's picture. And that powerful kangaroo-like tail, which is used for balancing. . . . See the leg in the photo? Lena's drawing picks that up too. Probably an injury from a trap. Am I correct, Lena? Was this photograph your model?"

I think I nodded. I tried to speak, but all I could manage was a sort of croak. No one laughed, though.

Later I was able to look back, the way you do with a dream that you try to catch before it dissolves. I was beyond excitement, beyond amazement at Dr. Hogg's mysterious power. Part of me wanted to jump up and shout that it was all a mistake, that it wasn't true. But I couldn't move. I barely noticed when the next report started. I didn't hear one word of it.

It seemed a long time later when I became aware of things again. I saw the kids, I saw Mr. Harris, I saw Dr. Hogg, all listening politely to how Pere David's deer, extinct in their original habitat, were thriving in captivity. I could tell that those thriving deer didn't mean all that much to Dr. Hogg. Not like my beast. Not like the thylacine that had been photographed more than fifty years ago standing in its cage, maimed and morose, the last of its kind ever seen.

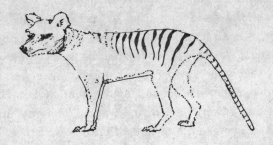

3   After that day at the Institute, I read everything I could get hold of about Tasmania, which wasn't much. Still less about the thylacine, except that everyone in Tasmania had had it in for my beast because it ate wallabies that the fur traders wanted. So thylacines were poisoned, trapped, shot, killed by dogs, until they were used up or else driven back into the wildest, thorniest part of Tasmania where there wasn't enough natural prey for them. Just as I had imagined, it turned out that thylacines had enormous appetites.

Anyway, I didn't have much time to get my report done. I strung out what I could, putting in all the bits Dr. Hogg had told us, and when I got to the end I just couldn't resist finishing with the words that had set the whole thing going. "Possibly," I wrote, "due to a few people whose names I am not at liberty to divulge, thylacine may once again be seen trotting doggedly after its prey or leaping over the rough terrain of its natural habitat." *Terrain* is a word I learned when I was reading about Tasmania, which has lots of it.

I got my report in just in time, and that was all there was to it. I thought about Dr. Hogg, though, and a couple of times on my way home from school I detoured past the Institute, which isn't far from where I live, and not far from the zoo either.

Then, just before spring vacation, Mr. Harris handed me a note from Dr. Hogg inviting me to visit her lab. Mr. Harris said he had sent along a couple of reports from the class project, and one of them had been mine. I felt a little funny when he told me this, but I wasn't worried. It never occurred to me that she might have a hidden reason for asking me. Maybe Mr. Blanc has a point about me needing to be more realistic. Looking back now, I'm amazed I was so simple-minded.

It was different being at the Institute without my class. Dr. Hogg seemed taller and quicker. There were spaces for me, but I didn't quite fit them. I kept going through doorways at exactly the same moment that she did, or finding my voice the instant she began to talk again.

She gave me a lab coat and a mask and showed me the nursery. They have attendants whose job is to baby the babies so they won't grow up unevenly. It made me wonder how that might work with people. Did Mr. Blanc think about things like that? But if no one was uneven, then he'd be out of a job.

When we went into the potto room and I saw that ball of fur with its great staring eyes, I reached out the

23

way I had done for the tenrec. This time Dr. Hogg grabbed my arm. The cage has a glass front, but there's a narrow space around the frame where you could reach fingers through, and she told me the potto could bite my finger to the bone. I had to show her I wasn't just any dumb kid that thinks if an animal is furry it can be cuddled. I explained that I'd thought it was a loris and that I had a loris friend at the zoo. "I mean," I said, thinking how Mr. Blanc would react to me saying I had an animal friend, "I've established a meaningful relationship with a slow loris at the zoo."

Dr. Hogg let go of my arm and told me the potto was a member of the loris family and that this particular specimen had a vicious temper. She said it tried regularly to bite the hand that fed it. She'd probably have to get rid of it, which was too bad, because she'd been hoping that the potto might provide some clues that would lead to the survival of an endangered relative, an especially fragile member of the loris family. "Sometimes," she said, looking right at me, "it may be possible to reverse the process of near extinction." I looked straight back at her. I didn't yet know what she was driving at. I wasn't even uncomfortable anymore. I said that the slow loris I knew had a wonderful disposition and that I got along with him beautifully and that she ought to have a nice loris like him to work with. And she nodded thoughtfully.

Then we went into her office. It isn't anything like Mr. Blanc's office. No walls on her desk, just jumble. It's full of what she's always thinking about. Over the book case are pictures of all the extinct species that were around until quite recently. You walk in, and all those reminders are facing you like warnings. The Great Auk and Steller's sea cow, a kind of zebra called a quagga, and a certain kind of wolf.

She asked me to tell her more about the slow loris. I looked down and saw my "Beast on the Brink" on her desk sticking out of the jumble. I felt hot and itchy. I talked quite a lot about Jerry, the way he would do things I asked him to, and how we understood each other.

Then Dr. Hogg went on about her work with the primates and why she has the nervous tree shrews. I could feel her words beginning to probe like long, competent fingers, but it took a while before I guessed that she might be putting together what I said about Jerry with what I'd written about the thylacine. And then I saw how she could suspect that I really did know someone or some place where there were rare animals being kept.

When she asked me if I'd like to come in during vacation and try to coax the slow loris to accept her so they could put it through some experiments, I said, "But the slow loris I know is in the zoo."

She said right back, "We might be able to borrow him for a bit. We need an animal like the endangered one, which we can't use for our studies because it's protected. We'd hoped the potto would work, but it's hopeless."

All I could think of was how shy Jerry the slow loris was. And how slow. If you tried to rush him, he just curled up and went still.

Dr. Hogg said, "If you could get the slow loris to adapt to the tests, it might give us answers that would enable us to save..."

Her voice sounded like when she read to us about the sea cow. I couldn't look at her. What she was saying was wonderful and awful all at the same time. No one had ever said anything like that to me before, that I could actually help in something so important. When she was finished speaking, I was all mixed up. I wiggled my big toe, which was caught in the hole in my sock. Finally I had to sit down and take my sneaker off to pull the sock free. When I looked up, Dr. Hogg was scowling again the way she had with that tenrec. What was she thinking? About the slow loris or about that source I mentioned in my report, the source I wasn't at liberty to divulge?

Finally I mumbled, "I'm not sure. I don't know if I should take advantage of my friendship with Jerry...."

26

Dr. Hogg nodded. Not a word about immature attitudes. No wall between us, none at all. Except, I realized, that she had the impression from my report that I might have some crucial information about a rare surviving thylacine.

She began to talk again, her voice quite low but stretched tight. "You'd have a week to see the loris through transition. Then our attendants would take over. Some of them are wonders with the animals. They're so good at their work that often we have to make them take turns to keep them from getting too attached to certain animals. It's like the nursery. The attendants must give the babies all the tender loving care they need; otherwise the babies wouldn't work out as research specimens. The attachment that forms between an attendant and an animal may be vital in getting that animal through some of our more difficult or demanding tests, but we are always careful to remind everyone involved that the animals are here to be used. What I mean is. . ."

But she didn't say what she meant, and I had an uneasy feeling that I didn't want to hear it. I thought how easy it would be to get Jerry to do whatever they needed to find out about loris behavior. "What if it takes longer than a week?" I wanted to know.

She shrugged. "Wait and see. In this game you never know what to expect." She tossed her head, and the pencil tumbled down. She caught it absently before it hit the desk.

I wondered if my hair was thick enough to hold a pencil like that. Then, looking up at her, I saw her begin to smile, to nod. The funny thing is I smiled back as if everything was all decided and I knew what I was doing.

4 Instead of going home, I headed straight for the zoo. I figured I'd need all the time I could get.

The zoo was crowded because it was the first day of spring vacation. Inside the Small Animal House the main aisle was jammed. On either side the small animals shrieked and whistled and jabbered from their cages. I know what those animals are like when there's only me and a few others from the zoo; they can still be noisy, but they're never so shrill and wild. It made me think of Dr. Hogg's tree shrews and what being crowded does to them.

Jerry was avoiding it all by twining himself around his tree trunk and being so still that he looked like something that had grown there. When I called to him, he turned his head without moving any other part of his

28

body. I wished I'd taken the time to visit him when I didn't have a favor to ask. His great, circled eyes looked down on me with sleepy wonder.

"Don't you recognize me?" I called up to him.

"Hey," said someone next to me. "That kid's talking to the raccoon. Maybe it was her pet and she had to give it to the zoo. They get nasty as they grow older."

"It's a slow loris," I corrected, "not a raccoon. And he's not nasty. Ever."

That was a mistake. I had to wait for the people around Jerry's cage to move on. Jerry waited too. Then he began to unwind. He seemed to be pulling himself inside out, all in slow motion, with his elastic legs swiveling to let the rest of him down.

"Night," he said in his soft twitter.

Jerry speaks so slowly that you have to fill in for him.

I guessed he was telling me to come back at night, so quickly I explained how badly I needed him. I had to rush everything, then stop and wait as people paused to look at him, then pick up and rush along again. I told him about Dr. Hogg and the potto and the Observation Room and that it would only take a week and I would be with him and it was in the cause of endangered species, including a close relative, a kind of loris that's so rare they can't get one to work with.

Jerry's eyes seemed to grow larger and larger. Without a word he began to flow up the tree trunk. I stared up at him. He looked more like a woolly bear caterpillar than a small primate from Madagascar. I thought of pleading with him, but how could I, with him so sad-looking and distant, and all the people so curious and close? So I walked away from him.

I was scuffing along one of the zoo walks that connect the different animal exhibits when I heard and felt a fluttering overhead. Shading my eyes against the sun, I watched the little auk alight near me. He was so small you might never have noticed him, a fat, black and white sea bird with the wisest eyes you ever saw.

"Jerry's not himself. You must have upset him. Did you?"

I should have answered more carefully, but after all, here I was after a long time away, and there wasn't so much as a greeting for me, only an accusation. I told the little auk that if Jerry had listened more carefully, he wouldn't have been upset. "Maybe it's too complicated for a simple primate like Jerry. And it's impossible to explain everything with all that racket and all those people eavesdropping."

"Why didn't you wait for closing time?"

I told the little auk the matter was urgent. I needed help. All the time I was speaking I was aware of the little auk's eye on me. I wished I was telling this to Winifred, even though she'd be interrupting all the time. Or Benjamin. Benjamin would be hearing me through the special membrane on the top of his head where his ancestors had had a third eye; Benjamin was a sensitive listener. But the little auk was different. Like Mr. Blanc, he didn't let you know what he was thinking. So after a while I didn't feel encouraged to go on. If he'd asked me something or clucked sympathetically I'd have thought of a lot more to say. But he just eyed me with his bright, dark eye, and I ran out of words.

"What can I do?" I asked finally.

"What were you thinking of doing?"

"I might speak to Winifred or Benjamin."

"Why?"

I felt pinned by his look. I flung my arms out. "Because they're good friends of his, that's why. He trusts them."

"And so?"

"And so," I nearly shouted with exasperation, "he'll do what they say."

The little auk was silent.

I was regretting this whole conversation. "Well?" I demanded. "Why don't you tell me what you think?"

"I was wondering," said the little auk, "what Benjamin and Winifred might have to say to him."

I was dumbfounded. It had never occurred to me that either of them would fail to see the need for Jerry to cooperate. "I'll go see Benjamin right now. As soon as I explain—"

"You'd better wait," said the little auk. "The Reptile House is even more crowded than the Small Animal House. The rock python is swallowing something. You can't get near the tuatara cage."

"All right then. After dark. Will you tell him I'm coming? Tell them? We can meet the way we used to."

The little auk fluffed his feathers and stretched his tiny wings. "You haven't been here for a long time."

"I know, I know." I didn't see what that had to do with anything.

"Things are different. You can't meet after dark."

"Can't? Why not? Is it locked cages? Between the two of us, we ought to be able to handle that. What do they all do if they can't go out at night and see each other? They must be dying of boredom."

"There are worse things to die from."

If the little auk was going to be difficult, I wasn't going to help him. I just stood there. I hoped I looked annoyed.

"Listen to me," said the little auk. "They can get out, but not after dark. The dark belongs to the Others."

"Others? What do you mean?" The little auk can be maddeningly secret when he wants to, but he looked so serious now that I really had to know.

"The Others are those who cannot share the night places with the rest of us. You people have a saying: Birds of a feather flock together. And so we do, somewhat. But we can mingle too, because we know our place or our flock or family. But the Others are like creatures made of feather, scale, and fur. There is no place for them here, so

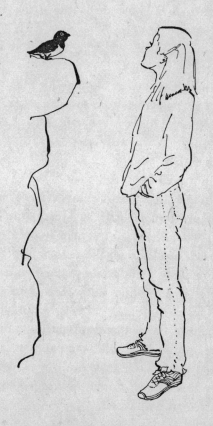

they keep moving, and the rules and boundaries that keep the rest of us in our place are not for them."

I felt like answering, What's so great about knowing your place? Or having only one place to belong to? But no one ever gets anywhere arguing with the little auk, so I changed the subject. "Couldn't we meet right after closing time, before it gets dark?"

The little auk cocked his head, considering. "Depends how long it'll take the aardvark to dig a hole for you under the zoo wall. You're bigger now, you know. That's a lot to ask of the aardvark during his only free time."

I nodded. "I can wriggle, though. I don't mind getting dirty."

"All right. Come after closing. We'll have some kind of tunnel for you across from the snack bar."

"Will you get all my . . . our friends?"

"I'll tell them."

"Jerry too?"

"I doubt he'll be in the mood."

I couldn't help feeling anxious. The little auk confirmed my own feeling that Jerry was going to be difficult. I would need all the help I could get.

I strolled out through the regular zoo gate wondering how to get my friends on my side. Benjamin could be counted on if I let him know I was in trouble. But Winifred loved fun and adventure. Maybe Winifred could be shown the challenge of getting a reluctant slow loris to take part in a vital campaign to save another endangered animal. Or maybe all of us together could give Jerry the kind of nudge he needed to come down from his tree all by himself.

5 They were already there on the steps of the Small Animal House when I slithered through the fresh tunnel under the zoo wall and ran to meet them. The platypuses looked like toys, their rubbery duckbills seeming stuck on. Winifred, her soft fur beaded with water from her pool, twirled with delight, spraying everyone else. Benjamin shrank from the wetness. He might have been a toy too, one well used, with his points a bit floppy and raggedy from the top of his head and down his back to the tip of his tail.

"You look different," squealed Winifred. "Your hair's grown. You're bigger."

I stooped and hugged her and Ernest; she was all over the place, but Ernest was reserved. Benjamin gave me a toothy grin, and I felt sorry I had stayed away from him so long.

The little auk kept glancing at the sky, which still

looked light enough to me, and muttering about getting down to business.

Winifred jumped from one step to another, leaving wet prints that showed the webbed shape of her paws. "Will we have an adventure?" she wanted to know. "Exciting things always happen when you come."

"Jerry might have a special adventure," I answered carefully. "That's what I need to—"

"Let's get him then. Why isn't he here?" Winifred scrambled up the steps.

"Wait," I called. I wanted to say things just right so that she'd understand, but the little auk said bluntly, "He won't come."

Winifred stared down her duckbill at us.

"I upset him," I told her before the little auk could get in another word.

Platypuses look puzzled even when they're not, because of the set of their eyes so close to their bill, but Winifred showed real puzzlement, and it came from deep inside.

"I didn't want to," I told her. "I needed help. I handled it badly. It could be wonderful and exciting. It's an opportunity. I couldn't get all that across to Jerry. Instead I—I'm afraid I scared him."

I could feel Benjamin taking all this in. I saw Winifred's eyes grow soft with concern. Only Ernest held out. Ernest and the little auk. Who said, "Maybe you'd better begin at the beginning. If you expect Winifred and Ernest and Benjamin to plead your case."

"It isn't a case." Then I stopped. I could tell that Winifred was taken aback by my sharpness. And Benjamin was sure to sense the little auk's mood.

"Lena wants Jerry to go to the Institute and be put in an Observation Room so she can show someone how good she is with animals."

"No," I protested, "it isn't like that. Really it isn't."

"It isn't?" said the little auk.

"Our Jerry?" said Benjamin.

"Away from here?" gasped Winifred.

The only thing left was to follow the little auk's advice and tell them everything from the beginning. It wasn't easy, especially after the way the little auk had put it. The story came out like a badly mixed cake, as though there were lumps under the surface that hadn't got absorbed properly.

And Winifred kept interrupting me. "When do we get to the adventure?" she wanted to know in the middle of why I was supposed to do my report on the Asiatic two-horned rhinoceros. "I need some excitement. You have no idea how dull it is now that our nights are spoiled."

"It's coming," I promised. "Just listen."

"Winifred's beside herself," Ernest remarked to the little auk. "She needs to get about more."

"I'm not beside myself," Winifred snapped. "I'm beside you. And have been for a long time. A platypus like me begins to long for something new, something exciting...."

"This thing with Lena may do her a world of good," Ernest went on in a low voice.

"Stop talking about me that way. I'm not sick, and you're not my vet."

Ernest turned to her. "I'm worried about you. All that talk about getting out is bound to lead to trouble."

SMALL ANIMAL HOUSE

38

"Well, I'm not about to spend the rest of my life in fear of something I can only smell."

All I could do was interrupt and plow my way through my story. This time I got pretty far, was already at the Institute being shown around, when Winifred piped up again.

"What sort of masks?"

"What?"

"On the animals. Do they hurt?"

"Of course not. The animals are very happy there."

"Except the tree shrews?"

"Yes. Right. Now listen, Winifred, I still have a lot to tell you."

"And the potto," she added. "I bet he's not happy either."

"Look, it's no one's fault. You have to understand that the tree shrews are extra sensitive to noise. They get nervous and then fat and then they won't breed. They're a special problem. And the potto is just bad-tempered. No one's—"

"And the tenrec," said Benjamin. "Don't forget that tenrec you mentioned. That won't wake up."

I sighed. "Yes, and Dr. Hogg's very concerned about it. She cares a whole lot. Benjamin, if you saw her, you'd feel her concern."

Benjamin said nothing more, so I picked up my story again. I went a long way with it. I was practically at the end. "You see," I said, appealing to Winifred, "how awkward it was for me. I felt so uncomfortable when Dr. Hogg was talking to me in her office."

"Why were you uncomfortable? Because you had to wear a mask?"

"Of course not. I told you masks don't hurt. Anyhow, I only wore one when I was in the nursery." My voice was rising. "Will you please forget about the masks?"

Then I stated very clearly that I felt guilty because I had led Dr. Hogg to think that I had some kind of inside information about a living thylacine. "Talking about Jerry just made it worse. It seemed to confirm that I had some connection with a secret refuge for animals that she didn't know about. So when she asked me if I'd like to help out over vacation with Jerry, well, what could I say?"

"You could say, 'No thank you,'" Benjamin offered.

"But you don't know Dr. Hogg. You can't say no to her. She cares so much. And she has this . . . commanding presence."

"Does that mean you have to do what she commands?" asked Winifred.

I didn't know how to go on. I had forgotten how very simple such simple animals really are. I began to feel it was hopeless, but I said, "It means you *want* to do what she says."

"How would that help about your report?" Ernest wanted to know.

"It wouldn't exactly help," I admitted, "but it would give me time. I could do something helpful for her while she still trusts me. Afterwards, well, of course I'll have to tell her the truth, that I made up that part of the report—"

"I thought you made it all up," Winifred put in.

"It's getting dark," said the little auk. "Not much more time."

"Right," I said. "We've got to talk to Jerry. Get him on our side. So he'll understand."

"Understand?"

"Yes, that he'll be contributing and I'll be contributing and Dr. Hogg will be able to move forward with her great work, so that by the time she has to be disappointed in me because I don't really have any inside information or sources about a thylacine, we'll all be farther ahead. All of us."

"I don't think so," said Winifred. She shook her head. "Not Jerry. He's . . ."

"He wouldn't like it somewhere else," Benjamin finished for her.

"But how do you know? I'd be with him every day. And something important might come of it. And then Dr. Hogg will understand that I didn't mean to trick her. I had no idea she'd ever see my report."

"But you're tricking her right now," Ernest pointed out. "Why don't you just tell her?"

"I can't," I wailed. "She'll hate me. She'll tell them at school. I'll spend the rest of my life behind Mr. Blanc's wall. Look," I said, trying to control myself, "I don't care if I get a D on my report, but what about Dr. Hogg's work on the rare endangered loris? She'll never get anywhere with that potto. And I'll never get anywhere either. She's offered me a kind of job. Not for money. But it's important. Vital. It's the first rung of the ladder. Think of all those endangered animals I might save in my career."

The platypuses exchanged glances. "I think. . . .We think maybe the most endangered animal just now is—"

"Oh, I know," I exclaimed. "It's the thylacine. If it still exists at all. But you can't stop working on other endangered species."

"Jerry," Ernest declared. "He's the one that's threatened. Jerry."

Winifred nodded. Benjamin sagged unhappily. The little auk peered upward.

"He's not," I shouted. "It could be an adventure. He could have fun while he's giving, I mean lending himself to science. He'd love Dr. Hogg. You should see her with animals. She thinks about them all the time. And when they need medicine or something, she invents ways to give it to them with tubes so they'll be handled as little as possible to reduce stress."

42

I caught the look the little auk was sending Benjamin. "Unless," I added hurriedly, "they like to be handled. Dr. Hogg has attendants who handle the babies and play with them. Not that Jerry would need medicine. They wouldn't even put him in with the other animals, because of contamination. See, she's very careful," I yelled. "She cares." I whipped past the little auk, flung open the door to the Small Animal House, and stomped in.

6 I hadn't noticed how dark it was getting, but now that I was inside I could see and hear the night. The nocturnal animals, eyes aglow, chittered and whistled and growled softly. Only Jerry was silent. He was hanging upside down on his tree limb. His eyes looked huge; they seemed intent on something minute and perilous straight ahead of him.

I tried to reach him with my voice. I could hear the platypuses padding up to me and Benjamin scuttling along on the concrete floor. I turned to them. "He's all tangled up in himself."

"That means he's unhappy," said Benjamin.

"Can't you help? Make him understand?"

The little auk, who had flown to the top of Jerry's tree trunk, said, "Maybe that's the trouble. Maybe he does understand."

"Let him speak for himself."

We waited. Beyond the night sounds of the animals, I heard a faint rumbling. Thunder? I looked up at the skylight. The rising moon was just clearing the edge of a cloud and lighting the aisle with pale stripes. Not thunder.

"Sleep," twittered Jerry. "People   Already   . More than slow loris   ." Bending backwards, he oozed his furry body upward until his eyes stared down between his hindquarters.

"What's he saying?" In the old days I would have understood, but now I was too pressed. You need to take your time with a slow loris, and Jerry's sentences were so full of holes. "What's he trying to say?"

"That he doesn't want to be studied," Benjamin supplied. "He doesn't want to be observed and measured."

"He said all that?" I was beside myself. I could feel the language we shared and that I'd always taken for granted slipping from my grasp.

"It's what he meant." There was a good deal of firmness in Benjamin's tone.

I felt defeated. And let down too by friends I'd counted on. Obviously we had grown apart. Or rather, they had stayed the same, but I had changed. Did growing up mean that I was growing away from them?

While I was thinking, the rumbling came closer and then suddenly stopped. A door slammed. A DOOR?

"Oh, no," cried Winifred. "The Others. We did stay out too late."

"Not the Others," said the little auk. "A truck."

"Oh," I gasped. "Oh, quick. They've come." I

bolted for the door, but I could hear voices bearing down on me from the other side. I wheeled.

"Who's come?" asked Benjamin, his points beginning to stick up sharply.

"For Jerry."

We all gaped at Jerry, who didn't move a muscle. The little auk swept across the aisle. "Over here," he directed. "The numbat cage. Everyone inside." I wrenched open the cage door. Except for one long-nosed numbat drowsing in the corner, the cage was empty.

Ernest held back. "Is it safe?"

"Of course," said the little auk. "The numbat sleeps at night." He pointed to a piece of rotten log crawling with termites. "All it eats are those insects."

I boosted Benjamin up into the cage and climbed in after him. Winifred and Ernest followed, and we all lined up against the back wall just as the door to the Small Animal House opened and two men walked in carrying a kind of crate.

"We won't turn on the light," said the uniformed one. "It'll only upset the animals. I can't understand why we have to do this tonight anyway."

The other one answered, "I told you. The boss said they need the animal right away. By first thing in the

morning." He stopped with his back to us and pointed. "That him?"

The man in the uniform started forward. "Don't. He doesn't like being handled by strangers. Let me." He held out his hand to Jerry. "Here's a grape for you," he called softly. "A grape. Come to me."

We could see Jerry untwist enough to begin, hand over hand over foot, to creep down until he was nearly level with the hand.

"Just grab him," said the man with the crate.

"Give him time. Usually I can coax him anywhere. Slide the box in underneath."

"I'm not getting paid overtime," the other man grumbled.

The one in the uniform was murmuring to Jerry, who stretched, one long-toed foot still firmly attached to the tree trunk, and reached out for the grape.

"What's that box for?" whispered Winifred. "What are they doing?"

"What I was telling you," I whispered back. "What I was trying to prepare Jerry for."

"You knew this was going to happen?"

"Ssh," warned Ernest.

"I didn't know it would be like this."

Benjamin said, "We've got to warn him."

But Jerry didn't need any warning. As soon as the strange man had moved partway into the cage, Jerry sprang back. All his fingers and toes clutched the limb.

"Pull him off," advised the stranger.

"Usually he trusts me." The man in the uniform sounded troubled and sad.

In an instant two gloved hands reached up and

grabbed Jerry, one going round him, the other plucking a foot from its grip on the limb. "Get his hands," ordered the stranger.

And all at once Jerry was transformed from the slow, furry creature we knew into a ferocious beast. He chittered. He screamed. His head darted at the gloved hands as if it were separate from his body. His lips were drawn back, his sharp teeth snapping and clicking. The thick gloves seemed to be everywhere, attacking him and prying him loose. Screeching, he lunged at those gloves so hard that one hand let go.

"Oh, stop them," cried Winifred.

"Hush," the little auk told her. "We will, but we can't do anything now."

I jumped forward, but the little auk fluttered into my face and forced me back. "They'll hurt him," I whispered. "They shouldn't pull him like that."

Benjamin called out, "Let go, Jerry, let go."

All the small animals, not just the nocturnal ones, were aroused, their screams adding to the din.

"Careful," said the man in uniform. "Don't squeeze too hard."

"You be careful. You should wear gloves. There, grab that hind foot."

Gradually Jerry's resistance was broken. His grip was tremendous, but the men kept at him until at last he was lifted free, his legs and arms extended like a puppet's, his fingers and toes clutching the air. In that terrible moment no one but me noticed that at the same time that Jerry was shoved into the crate, another animal was hauled out by the gloved hands and left clinging to the bars in the darkest corner of Jerry's cage.

Even after the truck had driven away, the small animals kept up their frenzy. Only the numbat reacted differently. "What are you all doing here?" it kept asking. It poked its long snout at Benjamin. "Pleasse," it snuffled, "I think you're sssquatting on my sssnack."

Benjamin was too dazed to respond. I shoved him toward the cage door. The numbat jerked forward, its tongue flicking out and in again.

We trailed out in single file, no one speaking, no one hurrying. Once we were all outside together, I had to break the awful silence that held up the picture in our minds of Jerry being manhandled like that and carried away. I said, "What a relief." I said, "All that racket in there." I could hear how callous I sounded, but there was no way to explain to Benjamin and Winifred that I was just trying to keep us going till we could collect our thoughts. Animals don't handle things that way. They don't care about appearances. When they're stirred up, you know it, and you might as well forget trying to reason with them.

Only I wanted to reassure them, to comfort them. How? By telling them that no one at the Institute was rough or uncaring? After what we had just seen, they would never believe me. I tried to hear Dr. Hogg's voice speaking of loving, tender care, but Jerry's screeching still echoed inside my head. "He'll be all right," I told them. "I just know he will. And I'll see him first thing tomorrow. He'll be fine." They wouldn't even look at me. They had nothing to say.

I started to walk away. I told them good night. I told them I'd come back and report to them about Jerry. I told them not to worry.

As soon as my back was turned, I heard the little auk say, "It's beyond us now. Out of our control."

"The Queen?" asked Winifred.

"You can't go to the Queen out of order," Ernest reminded them. "Aunt Martha would never stand for that."

"I'm afraid," said the little auk, "that this may be a matter for the Others."

"The Others!" gasped Winifred.

"But why?" demanded Benjamin.

"How?" asked Ernest.

"I don't know exactly, but I guess it's up to me to find out. You see . . ." The little auk's voice dropped. I could hardly hear him now. "There's more to this," the little auk was telling them, "more than any of you could imagine."

I kept on walking. Darkness settled like smoke on a still evening. Even the snack bar was growing indistinct, and the light gray pavement seemed to be sinking out of sight. I hardly noticed, though. Somehow I would reach the tunnel under the wall and come up on the other side where there would be lights and people and the subway station at the end of the street. Maybe then I would stop seeing Jerry, rigid and raging, suspended in the air by those thick-gloved hands.

7 I think that next day at the Institute was the worst day of my life. Maybe because I expected so much. Maybe because it started out so well, with me being given my white coat and a key, in case I wanted to show up before the place opened, and, best of all, a camera to use whenever anything unusual took place that I might want a photographic record of. I was supposed to get some practice with it the first day.

But after that super start, nothing happened. I mean absolutely nothing. Dr. Hogg was busy with that tenrec, which she believed was on the verge of waking, and after I was set up in the Observation Room with a chair and a little table, she never came near me. Once during the morning her secretary stopped by to ask if I wanted a drink or something. But nothing else happened. I had brought a sandwich, and by ten o'clock I was so bored I ate half of it. By noon my paper bag was empty.

As for Jerry, nothing I said or did made the slightest impression on him. I even wondered if he *was* Jerry. But then I remembered the night before. I had seen him carried out of his cage, the potto left there in his place. After what he had gone through I could hardly blame him for freezing up like this. Besides, he probably blamed me for what happened.

Of course I explained. Explained and explained to him. But he might as well have been stuffed. Not a muscle twitched.

Early in the afternoon the sun poured in through the one high window. It got so hot I thought of pulling off my shirt and wearing only the lab coat. But the lab coat isn't really my size, and it would have looked a bit odd if Dr. Hogg happened to come in. Finally I took it off. I pulled the chair up close to the glass front of Jerry's cage. I'd given up explaining. I was just waiting for him to come out of his sulk. I couldn't keep my eyes open. I tipped forward so that my forehead rested against the cool glass. I dozed.

I thought it was only a minute, but when I woke suddenly, snapping my head back, the sun had moved and the room was a little cooler. I felt awful, though. The tag end of a dream stuck to me like gummy sleep. Something about the tenrec. Only it wasn't the tenrec that had been asleep for nearly two years; it was Jerry. I looked up. He hadn't moved. "Oh Jerry," I whispered with a rush of gladness, "you're all right. You'll be all right." And my head sank back against the cool glass.

The next time I woke up I felt like swimming underwater. Everything was gray and dull. I was in no hurry. I liked the soft gray feeling against my skin.

53

Gradually I became aware of something touching my cheek. I held myself as still as I could. I tried to go on breathing slowly. I recognized that touch, and I didn't dare say a word.

Jerry's long, slender arm had reached through the narrow slot between the frame of the glass door and the corner bar of the cage. He had reached way around. His fingers groped, pausing at my ear, catching some of my hair, moving up and down as before. Then he spoke: "Where   Where are   you?"

I pulled back. Not because Dr. Hogg had warned me to keep clear of him till he was settled down, but to face him. I was so relieved. "Jerry," I said. "Jerry."

He waved his long middle finger like a spider reaching for a strand of its web. He was pressed up against the glass so that his rich fur was all flattened.

I called his name over and over. He stared sightlessly, confused and frightened. Or blind.

"Look at me," I begged. "Jerry, here. Right through the door."

"Can't see   you. Only me   here."

"But I'm here. In front of you."

"Where?   Where?   " His speech got slower and slower. Finally he curled himself into a tight knot.

I threw on my lab coat and went looking for Dr. Hogg. I told her secretary it was urgent. But when Dr. Hogg came and I said I was afraid that Jerry had been injured when he was taken from the zoo, I could see lines of annoyance around her mouth.

"I thought it was urgent."

"It is. Don't you see? He's blind."

She shook her head. "Not possible."

"But he can't see. He looked right at me, but he thinks he's the only one there."

"How do you know?" Her voice was level, dry.

"Because—" I looked at her, my mouth still open. What could I say? That Jerry had told me?

Then her voice warmed up. "I think we're up against the usual trauma of handling and changing quarters. I imagine the potto's just as upset to be on exhibit, since it actively dislikes people around it." Dr. Hogg shook her head. "I'm sure I've made it worse for both animals by rushing the move, but with only a week for you to take the loris through the transition, I couldn't risk losing any time. We've got to get him adjusted enough to begin the stress tests before you go back to school."

"Stress tests?" I had a lumpy feeling inside, the way I imagine the python feels when it swallows something whole.

"Yes. What we had the potto for. Except that it was too hyper-tense to go through them." I must have looked uncomfortable or something, because suddenly she gave me a smile and a brisk nod of encouragement. "It's going to be different now. With the loris already knowing and trusting you, he should be getting back to normal quite soon. So don't worry about him today."

Stress tests? I wanted to yell. What did she mean by that? What had I gotten into? What had I done to Jerry? But Dr. Hogg didn't stop, and she isn't an easy person to interrupt.

"Give him a little time and some breathing space," she was telling me, "and you'll be able to help ease him into the testing process. Just observe him for now. Jot down anything he does." She gave me a small pad with a hard cover. She gave me the pencil from her hair. She gave me a pair of bulky gloves and warned me not to touch the slow loris until he showed definite signs of recognizing me, and then to protect myself just in case.

I went back to the Observation Room to find Jerry still in his tight knot. I have to admit that after what Dr. Hogg had said, Jerry looked to me as though he was going through a stress test at this very moment. And failing it.

Still, Dr. Hogg who knew all about stressed animals believed that Jerry only needed a little more time. I fingered her long yellow pencil, then stuck it in my pocket along with the gloves and notebook and camera, which banged against my knee when I walked.

I felt weighed down with all that stuff, but I wouldn't have parted with a single ounce of it.

Then I went home to work on my hair.

8 I was so eager to get to the zoo that evening, it wasn't until I was actually there that I realized I had no idea how I was going to explain about Jerry. I decided to get everything said first to Benjamin, who isn't so quick to jump to unfair conclusions as Winifred or the little auk.

I marched past the python cage looking straight ahead in case the python was still swallowing. "I've come to pick you up," I announced to Benjamin.

Benjamin sank down the way he does when he's alarmed. "Pick me up?"

"Yes. I need to talk to you ahead of the rest. So come on."

"Not like last night? Jerry." Benjamin flicked his tail. "Jerry," he repeated. "How is he?"

"All right. That is, he's going to be all right. I mean,

he is now, except that he's not himself. Listen, I"ll explain if you promise not to tell Winifred and the little auk."

"Tell them what?"

So I went ahead and told him, except that I left out the part where I'd thought he was blind.

"Did you hold out your hands to him?" Benjamin asked me.

"I wasn't supposed to touch him. Dr. Hogg says he needs to calm down. She understands things like that."

"Did she give you those?"

I tried to follow Benjamin's glance. It wasn't easy, because while he only looks with one eye at a time, the pineal membrane on the top of his head takes in other kinds of things that regular eyes don't see. I finally realized it was the gloves he meant. I nodded. I tried to change the subject. I ended up taking Benjamin with me to meet the platypuses and the little auk.

They were just coming out of the Small Animal House as we reached the steps. Winifred poured out questions about Jerry. How badly had those men hurt him? Was he suffering? Were the terrible things they were saying in the Small Animal House true? Then she broke off. "Oh," she remarked, "You've done something else with your hair. What's that sticking in it?"

They all stared at me. I reached up and touched the rubber band I'd used when the bobby pins hadn't worked. I know my knot didn't look like Dr. Hogg's, but at least it still held the pencil.

"It's like a waterspout," said Ernest.

"What's that thing you're wearing?" Winifred demanded.

"It's my lab coat. Everyone wears them."

"What are those bulges over your knees?"

"Pockets. Equipment." I didn't like the way the conversation was going. Winifred was eyeing my bulging pockets with deep suspicion. So I tried to take the lead. I told them about Jerry's roomy cage and all his privacy. I felt Benjamin watching me. Quickly I added that of course on the first day Jerry's spirits were understandably low.

"Spirit?" interrupted Winifred. "Everyone in the Small Animal House is having a fit about Jerry's spirit. You'd better come in and tell them you've seen him."

The little auk whirred overhead. "Time to see Aunt Martha. We can't keep her waiting."

"But they're out of their minds in there," Winifred argued. "Just let Lena talk to them for a minute. Benjamin and Ernest can start for the elephant yard. Lena and I will catch up."

I followed Winifred up the steps and opened the door for her. It was a madhouse. Some animals ran in circles. Some flung themselves against the walls of their cages; some just stood up on their hind legs trembling violently. The numbat was sitting like that, bolt upright, hissing, "Imposssible sssituation." Across the aisle from him in Jerry's cage, at the tip of the tree, curled a ball of fur almost exactly like Jerry.

"Jerry," called Winifred.

"Sssh," hissed the numbat. "Don't encourage it."

"But that's not Jerry," I exclaimed.

"Hisss ghosst," the numbat told me. "Can't you tell? They've done away with Jerry, right? You were here lassst night. You sssaw. Well, thisss isss hisss ghosst, and we can't stand it, we sssensitive animals. Can't sssleep in a haunted houssse."

I laughed. "Why does everyone think it's a ghost?"

"It jussst isss," spluttered the numbat.

"I can tell you," Winifred broke in. "Because it's deathly still, except when suddenly terrible loud shrieks come out of its stillness."

"It'sss ssscary," put in the numbat. "Impossssible."

"But that's ridiculous. I know for a fact—"

"Still here?" The little auk cut me off. "Don't you know Aunt Martha's expecting us?"

"Aunt Martha can wait," Winifred told him. "These poor animals—"

"Aunt Martha may wait, but not the Queen. And certainly not the Others."

"Othersss?" said the numbat in a hush. "Oh, steer clear of those Others. Give them plenty of room. What they did to the kangaroo rats. A nice family, they were, the kangaroo rats. But you know how it isss. Ssso many small animalsss vying for this niche or that. Sssome of the pushier sssmall animalsss got it into their heads that kangaroo rats don't belong here. The poor things were ssset upon. They tried to ssshow that they belonged, but

61

they had to admit they were both rat and kangaroo. You can imagine what happened."

"No I can't."

"Never mind," said the little auk. "We must go."

"But what did happen?" Winifred pressed.

"They went away one night. The whole family." The numbat bunched itself into a compact bundle of stripes, but its long nose wagged nervously. "To the Othersss. And no one hasss ever ssseen them again." Its snout quivered. "You know, of courssse, that the Othersss don't live by the ordinary rulesss."

"You mean the kangaroo rats are with the Others now?"

The numbat's hiss dropped to a whisper. "If anyone knowsss, I expect it's the little auk. But around here the belief isss that they landed ssstraight in the clutches of the Devil. Ssso sssad. Sssuch a nice family."

"What I know," declared the little auk shortly, "is that we no longer have any choice. Some of us will have to go to the Others."

"Then it'll be like the kangaroo rats. You won't come back," said the numbat.

"Some of us will," the little auk promised as he led the way to the door.

"Don't you think we ought to straighten out the confusion about Jerry?" I began, but the little auk was in no frame of mind for any kind of delay. "I'll come back," I told the trembling numbat. "I'll come back and explain everything when we're done."

But the numbat only shook its head. "Don't be ssso sssure," it muttered. "Not if they take you to the Othersss."

Then I was out the door again and heading for Aunt Martha in the elephant yard.

9 The thing about elephants is that when you're away from them for a while you forget how really immense they are. I mean even their toenails.

I guess being with the small animals made it seem even stranger. All the way down the walk, past the fountain, and along the big zoo road, I had to watch every step because of the low-slung tuatara and the scurrying platypuses. It was a relief to have the little auk fluttering safely just ahead of us. So when we stopped and I found myself face to face with a low concrete wall holding bars thicker than my legs, I just stared.

Aunt Martha, shuffling back and forth inside her enclosure, stirred up dust and candy wrappers and muttered nervously. "There's something wrong, isn't there? I've felt it in my bones all day." She stopped. "Who's that with you? A girl?" Her ears flapped. "Do I know you?" she demanded. "You're bigger. Different."

There was something about standing before a

swaying elephant that made me come on stronger than I felt. "I'm glad you can see that," I began. "Maybe if these animals paid some attention to that, they would have got behind me preparing Jerry properly and no one would be upset."

"Who's upset?"

"Not that there's any reason for concern," I went on. Why did I have to explain myself to Aunt Martha? She had nothing to do with any of this. She just had this position in the zoo that made everyone be polite and consult her before they went before the lions. As far as I was concerned, all that meant was another delay and a lot of hot air.

"Who's upset?" bellowed Aunt Martha.

Benjamin scuttled out of range, but Winifred stood her ground and blurted, "Jerry was. He was terrified."

"Must you mention that slow loris? You know I can't stand furry creepy-crawlies."

"In that case," Winifred retorted, "maybe we'd better just go on over your head, straight to the Queen."

Aunt Martha straightened her trunk and blew at the tiny platypus, tumbling her against my legs. "None of that kind of talk, please. Over me, indeed. I can barely tolerate the likes of you at a respectful distance. Mind that you keep it."

The little auk stepped between us. He pointed out that this gathering was largely a matter of form. If Aunt Martha preferred us to go right to the Queen, we would be on our way. But Aunt Martha declared that she wasn't one to shirk responsibility, no matter how unpleasant. "And I feel in my bones," she grumbled, "that this will be unpleasant."

I thought it was some trick to feel anything through that thick, wrinkled hide, but I stayed polite and told her about everything that led up to Jerry's situation. I was doing my best, but Winifred wasn't taking any chances with me. "What about the tenrec that won't wake up?" she prompted at one point. And later, "Don't leave out about the tree shrews." I couldn't help being flustered by all her interruptions. To get it over with, I admitted that I'd agreed to work with Jerry before I'd asked his permission. I hadn't meant to upset him. I was just carried away because it was such a wonderful opportunity.

"No, no," said Benjamin. "You're all mixed up. It was Jerry that was carried away."

Well, what can you do with animals like Benjamin and Winifred getting in the way all the time? To make it worse, Aunt Martha took over, asking me whether I was aware of the consequences of misrepresenting those who could not speak for themselves, and when she ended up with, "Do you comprehend what you have done?" I was completely lost.

I struggled to find myself. I said, "I don't even know whether you're scolding me because it all started with me making up the Beast, or because I turned out to be telling the truth even though I didn't know it. I mean," I stammered, hoping to avoid the whole awful mess about tricking Dr. Hogg into thinking I knew something or someone that might lead to the whereabouts of a real live thylacine, "I mean, I didn't *know* I wasn't making that animal up." Of course I was hopelessly tangled. There was nothing to do but stop.

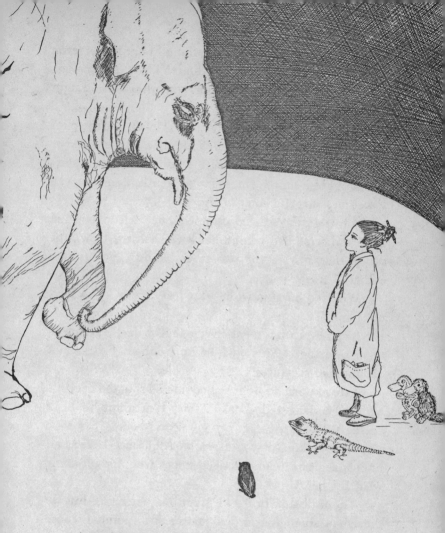

Aunt Martha's trunk stirred the dust in small circles. "Defiance," she droned, "will get you nowhere."

What was she getting at? I felt like curling up and going still. Maybe this was some kind of stress test to find out certain people limits. But Aunt Martha didn't look as though she was measuring anything about me or even jotting down notes, so it seemed more likely that she was as confused as I was and just throwing her weight around.

Benjamin, who was still trying to be fair, spoke up for me. "Lena's asking whether you mind because she lied or because she lied badly. At least, I think that's what she's asking." For a simple dinosaur-type reptile Benjamin can sometimes surprise you.

Aunt Martha seemed stumped. She curled her trunk back and scratched behind her ear. Then she blew little snorts that swirled the papers and candy cartons into eddies of trash.

Winifred burst in with, "But Jerry's why we're here, not Lena."

"Refrain from mentioning that name," bellowed Aunt Martha. "This girl is in trouble. Talk about endangered creatures!"

I stood up as straight as I could and shouted back, "I am not endangered. Look at me. I"m going to be a zoologist like Dr. Hogg. I'm going to rescue—"

"I'm looking at you all right. And what I see is an undersized girl in an oversized smock who doesn't know what fits her."

The little auk broke in. "You may be right, but we did come about the urgent matter of an animal whose name I won't mention."

"The child needs straightening out," Aunt Martha insisted.

"Meanwhile," continued the little auk, "maybe we'd better have a word with the Queen. I believe she's already been in touch with the Others."

Aunt Martha nodded her ponderous head. "The Queen next, of course. Each of us in our place. If only those Others had a proper place. I find it unsettling to think of them out there in the night. And such an odor. I don't know how any of the cats can bear being even slightly connected, but then I have an acutely sensitive nose." She curled her trunk and nestled it against her chest. "It's not right for someone of my stature to bridge the distance. Not fitting." Her small eye found me. "And I do know what's fitting," she added, "even if some people don't."

Winifred sniffed. "We less sensitive creatures will brave the smelly night then." Her webbed paw batted an empty peanut bag into the air, and she turned away after the little auk.

I thought about cutting out and going home. I didn't know what the little auk was up to, but I could tell he was still full of disapproval and he probably had some secret plan to surprise me with. The trouble, though, was that if I left now, I wouldn't be any farther ahead with Jerry. I needed these animals more than ever, and the little auk knew that I would have to go along with him.

Benjamin was scuttling hard to catch up to the platypuses. Suddenly he stopped and turned. "Coming?" he called to me. "I'll wait."

Naturally I ran to him. I knew he wasn't at his best at night. Yet here he was, unwilling to lose me and uneasy about being lost. We went on together. We had to cut across the grass. It was hard to see anything, and then we found ourselves on a real road that I didn't recognize.

I didn't know the building ahead of us either. It was a now-you-see-it now-you-don't kind of night, with lots of thick clouds massing and regrouping all the time. We came to a big sort of parking lot now. I could see a truck, a trailer, some covered mounds of something, and those huge bins for collecting trash and garbage. The platypuses and the little auk were already in the middle of the lot; they looked like pebbles in a moon crater.

Ernest was nervous. "Isn't this place off limits?"

"Quiet," said the little auk.

"What's that?" whispered Winifred.

We all turned at once, but we didn't know which way to look. Then a dark shape came gliding away from a pyramid of barrels, and a trickle of moonlight washed the shape with tawny light. I saw the furrowed face and deep golden eyes of a lioness.

"Girl," growled the lioness, "come here."

Benjamin flattened himself on the pavement. Winifred's duckbill pressed against my ankle. "I am here. With my friends." At my words the little animals flinched.

"You must learn to speak in the night voice," said the lioness.

"I'm not an animal."

"But you are. You are friend and enemy. You've put one of us in danger. When one is endangered, all are threatened. Do you understand?"

I said, "It's you animals who don't understand. There are people who can help endangered species. All right, I made a mistake getting Jerry rushed off to the Institute, but—"

"Jerry?"

"The slow loris. The reason I'm here."

70

The yellow eyes gleamed. "You think you know why you're here."

"Better than ... better than Aunt Martha," I finished carefully.

The lioness said, "You are here because we have decreed that you must be. As for Aunt Martha, her kind has worked so long with people that she tends to think like them. She believes in rewarding right and punishing wrong."

"And you don't?"

"Survival," growled the lioness, "is what we believe in."

I squared my shoulders, forgetting that this gesture wouldn't be very noticeable inside my big lab coat. "So do I," I declared. "So does Dr. Hogg. We're trying to do something important. Every animal here seems set on making that as hard as they can. So what can I do?"

"Do?" purred the lioness. "Listen. Look."

I heard rustlings, padded footsteps. I saw moving forms slink behind the trailer; I saw shadow shapes settle on the ground like sphinxes. Then, on top of the covered mound, one long, high-shouldered form stood up full length, its great curving tail just clearing the bundled hill. It turned its small head toward us, but it didn't look at me. Yet it seemed to find something it was looking for, because a moment later it bounded to the pavement and walked, stiff-legged, to stand beside the lioness. Now I could see its deeply lined face, its lovely mottled coat.

A low growl rolled out of the darkness. A maned lion crept out from under a trailer. "I could handle this. We don't need Cheetah."

The lioness began to twitch her tail. "No, Regulus. We have trouble enough."

A small cub pranced out behind the lion and pounced on the lioness's switching tail. Regulus snarled at it. Ignoring him, the cub caught the tail, rolled onto its back, and boxed with fat paws at the tufted end. Regulus cuffed the playful cub and sent it mewing back under cover. "Just remember," he told the lioness, "Cheetah has served people as long as elephants have. Can we trust an animal who wears a collar and hunts for a master?"

The cheetah turned its small, lined face toward the massive lion, but its look seemed to go right through him.

"My son," said the lioness, "don't be deceived by appearances. Through all the ages of its captivity, Cheetah has kept the secret of its own life." She turned to the cheetah. "You can see that we have taken the matter as far as we can. Are you ready?"

The cheetah's voice was smooth as glazing. "I can't go much farther. I'm not that different from you."

"Different enough," rumbled the lioness. "In you two distinct animal types mingle. You hunt alone. The dog in your catness brings you closer to the Others than we may venture. The girl must go with you."

I was beginning to think I should never have come here. "Go where?" I blurted.

"To the edge. To the distance."

"Look," I told her, "are you sure this has something to do with what I'm here for? I'm trying to find a practical solution to a particular problem, and now you expect me to go with this cheetah to some vague place you won't even tell me about."

"It is a risk. We have considered that."

"Then tell me, where is this distance?" I didn't see how she could be referring to one cheetah's territory, which I know from what Dr. Hogg said has to be awfully big. There was something ominous about the kind of distance that was no actual place, that you couldn't define with boundaries like walls and streets and buildings. "I can't stay all night, you know. I've got to get home before my parents do. Maybe I don't want to go near any edge."

The cheetah faced me. "Our distance is shrinking, vanishing. The edge is blurred and perilous."

The cheetah's gaze held me. I felt myself reaching out and down, seeking someone familiar and known and definite.

"Choose one companion if you like. It may steady you."

I was glad to turn away from those eyes. My glance fell on Winifred first. She tipped her furry head, her duckbill set at an angle that made her look silly and useless. "I'm feeling a bit nervous," she informed me. "I get the giggles when I'm nervous." She didn't have to tell me that she didn't want me to choose her. The little auk was, of course, the wisest of them all, but so far that hadn't done me much good. Then there was Benjamin, who wasn't wise and wasn't clever, but who waited for me like a true friend. "Benjamin," I said. "He's been around for so long, for so much longer than the rest of us."

"He keeps cool too," Winifred offered.

I nodded. "So will you, Benjamin?" I could see his low-slung body sinking even lower. "I think they understand that I can't spend much more time here. It shouldn't take long."

He dragged himself over to me. "I'll try. But if Cheetah forgets I'm invited—"

"Say no more." The lioness drew back, her skin rippling with distaste. "Come no closer. Listen. Look."

Benjamin squatted very low. I could tell he felt unhappy about the Queen not being able to stand having him near her. He was sort of trying to disappear.

Only it was the lioness who slipped off into the darkness. All the animals whose eyes had gleamed out of the night were drawing back as well. The cheetah had declared that the distance was shrinking, but right now it felt exactly the opposite. The presence of those animals had closed in around us, their eyes and breath holding off the empty reaches of the night, the hugeness of the black sky. I wished they were still here, surrounding me, but I knew we were alone in the delivery area with its edges blurred. In all this space there was only one stiff cheetah, one small, loyal tuatara, and me with my hair still up and the pencil in its knot and the gloves and camera in my pockets making dents in my knees.

10 The cheetah set a zigzag course that confused me and tired Benjamin. After a while I called out, "Wait." The cheetah went still. "You're too far ahead," I complained.

"It is the way of the cheetah. We are made on the edge of our kind. We must keep our distance or perish." It started off again. "The tuatara understands," it called back to me. "All creatures understand, except your kind."

"Come on, Benjamin." I picked the tuatara up in my arms. "I don't know where this is going to get us, but it can't hurt to follow him a little longer." But I thought to myself: I do so understand. I know about how cheetahs can't breed and raise their young unless they have lots of space or distance or whatever you call it.

The clouds had blown clear again. Benjamin's points stood straight up at the sight of an old stone building where the cheetah was heading.

"What is it?" I whispered.

77

"The Old Lion House. It's all broken down inside. Only the Others may go there."

"Benjamin, just exactly who are the Others?"

Benjamin shook his heavy head. "We don't know for sure. Only that they aren't like the rest of us here. They have no place in the zoo. They leave their scent on every path they tread, and you know simply that it's different. You can't say: Here went tigers, or here went wolves, here went bears. They are one thing, and yet another as well. The little auk says they are outside the rules and would prey on us and even on each other if the need drives them to it."

I didn't like the sound of that. I didn't like what I could see of the Old Lion House. I tried to stall. "Isn't it out of bounds?" I called ahead to the cheetah.

The cheetah pivoted. "Don't press me," it snarled. "Of course it is out of bounds. The risk is great. The time is short. And," it finished, catching its breath, "I tire of my companions."

But I still didn't like the look of that tall, rough building that loomed like a fortress ahead of us. "It's just the Old Lion House," I whispered, hugging Benjamin to me. I stared up at its forbidding face of stone, its high, deep-set window, the tremendous stone block over its arched entry. "It's like an old castle."

The cheetah mounted the steps, its bony shoulders seeming to shrug as it led us through that entry and into the gloom of crumbling walls, broken glass, collapsed beams. Only the tiles that line the inside cages were still intact. In the pale light that filtered through the burned-out roof they gave off a dull, cold sheen.

I stared through the inner doorway at the clutter, at skeletal ribs that spanned what was left of the ceiling. Bats swooped down from them and winged over our heads. I turned off into a side room where I saw a sink ripped from its mounting, pipes twisted and coated with slime. There were bins and cages beyond a closet that held blackness and a horrible smell. That smell was everywhere, but worse where it was contained like that. I banged against an old refrigerator door that was dangling from a single hinge; it creaked and swung and tipped back into the darkness.

"Why . . . why are we here?" I whispered.

"Look." The cheetah's voice flowed from somewhere inside the main shell of the building. "Listen."

I carried Benjamin through the inner entrance and set him down on the floor. Then I gasped. All the tiled cages that I had glimpsed before held the strangest animals, all of them watching me.

Benjamin stood motionless.

"What is it?" I whispered to him.

"Can't you smell them?" was all he said.

"Where's the cheetah?" My voice sounded funny, sort of ragged.

"Look," growled the cheetah from above. "Listen." There it was, stretched full length on a kind of shelf in one of the cages. "This is where I was kept before the new lion house was built."

"But you can't even stand up there."

"Neither could the lions and tigers and panthers. Yet all were here. It is where the zoo people said we belonged."

I pointed to the row of cages. "And did these animals live here too?"

"No. The zoo had no place for them at all. The zoo cats shunned them; the dog family denied them. They have never belonged."

"Then what are they doing here?"

The cheetah sprang down from the narrow shelf. "You have brought them."

"But how could I? I don't even know them."

"You have brought them because of what you dreamed up in your report, and because you used the slow loris."

"You mean I imagined them?" I squealed. All the animals started, then froze. "Are you saying they're not real?" I tried to hold my voice steady. I wished I could remember what Mr. Blanc had said about keeping a handle on reality.

The cheetah flattened its ears and gazed at an animal with a head like a weasel, but with huge eyes and coarse whiskers and bearlike ears. "This fossa is real, and though it is more cat than any here but me, still it is not cat enough to be considered one."

The fossa turned its close-furred face away from me and lashed its long tail.

"It hates to be looked at. It has come only because it must, so that you will believe. If you can believe in this fossa and in these Others who have come for you, then you may accept what we are forced to show you." The cheetah paused. "Look well. All are real, as real as the slow loris which you tried to use as though it wasn't real. You will see that you endangered much more than even you could ever imagine."

"All right. So that's an animal called a fossa. But I'm not the kind of person who needs to be shown it. You should see my school guidance counselor, if you think I'm hard to convince."

The fossa curved its tail, padded like a bear to the cage opening, and jumped heavily to the floor. As it passed, my nostrils filled with a burning smell.

"Now this small-eared dog," the cheetah remarked, showing me a foxlike animal that moved like a cat, "is next in catness."

The small-eared dog paced, lithe and silent, its eyes deeply glowing. A long-bodied animal sharing its cage rose on stumpy legs, but without that catlike grace. "There's more to life than catness," it whined. "What other half-dog can dive like an otter?"

From the adjoining cage a long-necked, humpbacked creature uttered a shrill laughing bark. "Listen to the common bush dog." It thrust its sharp face through the bars at me. "I have the distinction of being the least like everyone else here. Except," it added, "for you two."

A heavy-bodied animal at the end of the row raised a huge, rat-shaped head. "Aardwolf!" Its massive jaws

opened, its sharp teeth clicked. "Aardwolf, even with your foul preference for insects, you're not all that different."

"Oh," I gasped, "what is that?"

"She, not *that*," corrected the cheetah. "*She* is a Tasmanian devil."

"I have the distinction," yapped the aardwolf, "of living longer on the brink—"

The devil's pink ears stood out like two delicate shells from her dense black and white fur. "Are you going to let that weak-brained aardwolf go on like that?" she complained to the cheetah. "He can't forget himself for an instant. It's a good thing his kind has been protected so long. He'd give his own pups away out of sheer boastfulness."

The cheetah turned to the devil. "We are here to share a risk together, as we have been doing separately each night for the sake of one in absolute peril. What difference does it make where each of us prowls? We're all on the edge."

"Look at the hog-badger," the Tasmanian devil muttered to the aardwolf. "You won't see him bragging. Mostly you won't see him at all."

The aardwolf's sparse mane bristled. "Devil," it growled.

The cheetah ignored them. "It is time. Where's the raccoon dog?" it asked.

An animal with the legs of a fox and the face of a raccoon slipped between the bars of another cage and trotted nimbly along the gutter till it was across from us. "Follow me," it barked.

"Where to?" I wanted to know.

"The stairs. And partway down. You'll need to look and listen with all your might, because you'll have just one moment. It's all we dare risk."

I stumbled into the splintered frame of a long wooden crate, then picked my way around it. Benjamin scrambled after me. The raccoon dog, already poised at the entrance to the little room by the doorway, warned us that there was worse clutter ahead. Benjamin kept bogging down in crumbled lath and plaster. I tried to shove aside a bin that blocked my way to the stairwell and found myself wading through piles of thick, wired glass. I reached back for Benjamin and set him on the landing. "I think I'll have to go backwards, like climbing down a ladder," I whispered. "You wait here."

I started to let myself down. One foot crashed through something, and I couldn't go on. I turned carefully, leaning back and hooking my arm around a pipe. All I could make out were the small night eyes of the raccoon dog. Then, gradually, as I kept on staring, I saw that it was dimly lit at the far end of the cellar. There was no wall there. It looked as though that part of the building had been sliced off.

And now I could distinguish various levels and surfaces. The long wall across from me, for instance; it just crumbled away where it reached that open end. As my eyes moved in from the pale light, I could make out a kind of rocky mound sloping toward that long wall. Something shiny, bright-dark, lay below the mound toward the center of the cellar. Could it be water? It looked like a still, black pool.

Now that I was getting my bearings I could see that this whole underground area was merging with the outdoors. Branches had entered through the opening at the end; vines had taken hold and had spread as far as the ledge; gnarled roots, grown inward, seemed to prop up the whole building. And from the maze of cylinders and ducts that dangled from the ceiling, tendrils and wires coiled together and lashed themselves to the frayed ends of light cords.

Suddenly the raccoon dog whimpered. Then it growled and dodged past me.

"Is it dangerous?" whispered Benjamin as the animal brushed past him as well.

"Of course," snapped the raccoon dog. "It always is." It scrambled to the alcove and was gone.

Dangerous! I groped in the dark for something, anything that might protect us. What I ended up with was a jagged slab of that heavy glass reinforced with wire mesh. I raised my arm, ready to hurl the glass if necessary. The glass caught some of the dim light from below; it had a greenish tinge. I waited.

I heard something stir in the blackness at the near end of the cellar. It coughed. I stared and stared till I could see sparks inside my own eyes. Then, just when I couldn't stand waiting any longer, an animal stepped across the floor below, skirted the pool, and climbed partway up the ledge. When it was almost as high as I was, it turned. It turned, and I could see its wolf head, its pale unblinking eyes, its long sloping back that merged — just like my drawing — into a straight, stiff tail.

I don't know how long I held my breath, how long I stared. But my mind worked for me. It made me reach down into my pocket and grasp my camera. As I moved, the animal showed its teeth. It made a sound that was part snarl, part cough. The strange thing is that I recognized that sound; I'd never heard it, of course, but I knew it from everything I had read about thylacines. That was when it really hit me: I had heard a *thylacine*, a Tasmanian tiger!

Slowly, carefully, I raised the camera. I aimed as best I could, right at those staring eyes, and I pressed the trigger. The flash was blinding. It smelled hot. I heard a long, stuttering bark, but when I could see again, there was nothing there but the ledge and the pale light where the cellar opened out at the far end.

11 I went crashing up the stairs. I was so excited I nearly forgot Benjamin. But I stumbled just where I'd left him, and that brought me up short. I swept him up in my arms.

"Oomph," he grunted.

I loosened my grip, and he swung his head gratefully. "Where is everyone?" I whispered as I carried him into the main part of the building. "Cheetah!" I yelled. "Cheetah, where are you? Where's the raccoon dog?" I peered everywhere, through to the alcove and the doorway out, down the length of the great room with all its rubble and its solid wall of cages, all empty. I stood in the midst of crumbling crates and splintered glass; nothing stirred, nothing breathed.

Except Benjamin, who said, "What happened?" just the way someone does after they've dropped off to sleep and then suddenly woken up.

"I thought.... I'm not sure." And really I wasn't. What I'd seen was like a vision, a dream; it had lasted only a split second. How could it have been real? How could any of those Others have filled these empty cages? Maybe there was something about the stale air in here that put queer notions in your head. "I thought I saw ... something," I finished lamely.

And then Benjamin tensed. At first I thought it was because of what I'd just said. In the next moment I knew that he sensed something that I couldn't see or hear. I held still. I listened and I looked.

Somehow I could tell, even before setting eyes on it, that the cheetah was padding in through the doorway. Then I turned to watch it weaving silently around the obstacles, touching nothing, till it came to a standstill.

The cheetah moaned, "Too late, too late." It stared straight at me.

"What's too late?"

"Don't you know?"

I shrank from its tone.

"Don't you know what you've done?"

"Was I dreaming?" I whispered. "Those Others....? And then, underground.... Only it was so dark. Dark, and you could imagine...."

"There was a light," said Benjamin. "A flare."

I swallowed. My hand reached down below Benjamin to my pocket. I could feel the camera there. "A flash, yes," I said. "Because I saw a thylacine. *A thylacine.* I took its picture." I stood there waiting for the cheetah to tell me I was out of my mind.

Only the cheetah simply moaned again.

"Then where is it?" I demanded, the excitement

surging up again. "That thylacine, where is it? And where are those Others?"

"Gone," said the cheetah. "Too late. Thylacine was terrified. Of you."

"But I didn't do anything to it," I blurted. "I mean, I picked up something to throw, just in case. Well, the raccoon dog said it was dangerous. . . ." I turned from the cheetah's burning look. "At least I had the presence of mind to remember the camera. Isn't that wonderful?" I appealed to Benjamin. "You understand what this means, don't you? What this means? Dr. Hogg will be so thrilled. Nothing else will matter. It's fantastic."

The cheetah demanded, "And is it wonderful that Thylacine is probably in the most dangerous place of all?"

"Where's that?"

"Wherever people are. He was seen heading straight for the wall where the aardvark made the hole for you."

"Never mind," I answered. "Dr. Hogg will get him."

"She'd only drive him to his death."

"She'll save him."

The cheetah said, "Can you still be so blind?"

I shook my head. "But you brought me here. To show me—"

"So you would see. We had to risk showing Thylacine to you before you made up something that would put your Dr. Hogg on his track. You had to be shown how close it was."

"But somebody has to know he's here," I insisted. "Otherwise he wouldn't be." But looking at the cheetah, I wasn't so sure of that. "Then how . . . ?"

"Be still," commanded the cheetah. "I will tell you now. You will have to know."

"You could have told me before," I retorted, "and maybe saved—"

The cheetah cut me off with a snarl. "You would not have believed."

I started to snap back, but the cheetah's look changed my mind, and all I did was grumble about the secret network of people that ought to be in touch with Dr. Hogg if they were really serious about saving animals like the thylacine.

"There are no people," said the cheetah. "And the more you speak, the less I trust this telling."

How could there be no people involved? I opened my mouth, then shut it again.

There was a pause. The cheetah seemed to be testing me. One false word, and I would hear no more. The cheetah's tail switched; slowly the lithe body sank to its haunches. "The Tasmanian devil," it began, "is a pouched animal. It carries its young like the kangaroo, the possum. Like the Tasmanian tiger, the thylacine. You saw a Tasmanian devil in the cage here. She is the black furred creature with the white markings and the pink ears."

I nodded. I would never forget that animal, never forget her great snapping jaws.

"Tasmanian devils are savage hunters," the cheetah went on, "but also scavengers. Once it was their habit to follow the hunting thylacines, to clean up what they left. Till the thylacines were all but killed off. The devil you saw here came from Tasmania, where she was fortunate—or maybe unfortunate—to attach herself to one of the last of the thylacines, one that had two infants newly out of her pouch."

"Baby thylacines? Real, live—"

"The mother thylacine found poisoned bait and—"

"How could baby thylacines survive if their mother was poisoned?"

The cheetah snarled. "You fling your questions across the path of my telling." Its eyes half closed as if to shield itself from the sight of me. "That voracious devil," it went on, "had just weaned her own young and still had milk. Even though she saw the thylacine stagger away from the bait, the devil couldn't refrain from tasting it too. Then she heard the hunters who had set the bait. She managed to crawl as far as the dead thylacine's nest.

"If the devil hadn't been sickened by the poison, probably she would have eaten the two infant thylacines waiting for the mother who would never come. As it was, the clumsy devil just collapsed there, accidentally smothering one of the thylacine's babies. Its brother crawled into the devil's pouch and began to nurse. That made the milk keep coming. When the hunters found the devil still alive, they crated her, sick as she was, to ship her to a zoo. By the time she reached here, she had taken over the care of the orphan thylacine."

"But how could she? Thylacine's so much bigger."

The cheetah shut its eyes for a moment. "It didn't work out very well. Thylacine kept falling out of the devil's pouch, or tottering off. It's the way of thylacine young to leave the pouch quite early. The devil nearly lost her mind trying to keep track of him. She got so distraught we thought she might kill him."

"Kill him! Why would she do that?"

"She is short-tempered and powerful. Usually she kills because she must, but sometimes out of sheer frenzy. We nearly lost an entire family of kangaroo rats because of her."

I gasped. "Nearly?"

"We saved a few. A narrow escape. Those little animals didn't know enough to keep out of her way. She was in a terrible state at the time. Thylacine wouldn't even stay in the lair the zoo had given her. Sooner or later he was bound to be seen."

"But how can you be sure he wasn't? Maybe some sharp, dedicated—"

"Do not cut me off again." The cheetah's head was so low it seemed to be stalking. "The Others had to take charge. They were already outcasts, leading lives apart from the other zoo animals. Until Thylacine's predicament forced them to come together, they had led their solitary lives in secret, whether caged or lurking in the zoo's forgotten places. Sometimes they banded together to raid one of the exhibits, trying to make a place for themselves, pushing some other unwary species outside, into the distance. Mostly, though, each kind kept to itself and posed little threat to the more sociable zoo animals going about their business after hours. But Thylacine's plight brought them together. They made a den for him here in the cellar of the Old Lion House. At first only the devil came nightly to nurse him, but later the Others took turns bringing food. Poor devil, she was jealous. But Thylacine was too much for her. She was forced to let the Others share in his upbringing."

94

The little auk whirred in through the arch. "They've lost him," he called. "They're returning for orders."

The cheetah's face lines deepened. "We must think where thylacines go when they're frightened."

The little auk said, "You must think where a thylacine would go who's been raised by a raccoon dog and a devil and a fossa and all the Others that are at least two different kinds in one. Thylacine's a combination of a lot more than any one of them."

"You knew!" I cried. "All the time I was telling you about Dr. Hogg and everything, you knew."

"It was a secret," said the little auk.

"But you could have spared us all so much."

"That didn't give me the right."

I looked down at Benjamin. "Did you know too?"

"Only that something important and dangerous was here. I smelled the Others, but I never saw them. Only now I've a feeling I must have seen Thylacine trotting over by the bear dens once."

"Thylacine runs every night," said the little auk. "The darkness makes him restless, so he trots for hours around the zoo grounds. He doesn't understand the limits here or his own limits or anything."

"He doesn't understand who he is," added the cheetah. "From the beginning everything was wrong. The devil was always snapping at him one moment and crooning at him the next."

"Then how can you possibly figure out where to look for him?" I demanded. "Let me get help."

The cheetah jutted its bony shoulders. "Come tomorrow. We may yet need one of your kind."

"Then let me bring—" I choked back the rest of my plea. The cheetah's wrinkled muzzle and clenched face line spoke for it. I gathered up all my courage and tried one more time. "But you admit you may need me, and I'm a person."

"An edge person," the cheetah answered. Its small face was smooth again, like its tone. "Don't you know that yet? You are in between, like us, like the Others. You speak our language and that of people as well. That is a gift that brings you to the edge of your being. So does your imagination, which gives you the power to create and to destroy." The cheetah's cold eyes made me shiver. "You should learn wariness. Before it's too late."

Without a word of parting, it spun around and disappeared into the dark passage.

12 The next morning I couldn't wait to get to the Institute. I knew I mustn't say anything to Dr. Hogg, but I just hoped that somehow I could get across to her that something wonderful and almost unbelievable had happened. I was sure that as soon as Thylacine was found, I could convince Cheetah and the Others to let her help. She would show them all, especially the little auk, that certain dedicated people can be trusted.

As I walked along, I thought up one way, then another, for breaking the news to her. Was I also thinking that now she'd never have to know about how I made everything up in my report? I really don't think I cared about that. I mean, it wasn't what mattered just then, wasn't what made me smile to myself. I walked, had my hands, or at least my fingertips, in my pockets. I felt the gloves. But I could just reach the loop that's attached to the camera. And I imagined pulling it out with a sweep and presenting it to her with my news.

"Well, hello there."

Looking up, I had to squint into the sun. But I already recognized Mr. Blanc's voice. He was walking a bike. He didn't look anything like school. I felt like shouting, "So there, so there!" like a little kid.

He wiped his sleeve across his forehead. "Pretty early for a vacation morning, isn't it? Where are you off to?"

"To work."

"Work." It wasn't a question, but the way he said it was full of questioning.

I pulled up my gloves. I hauled out the precious camera. "I'm helping out at the Institute for the Study of Endangered Species," I said.

I could tell from the way he looked at me that he was going to check up on that.

"Why aren't you riding your bike?" I asked him.

"Dogs."

"Dogs what?"

"Dogs bad on this street. They chase me."

"So you're taking the bike for a walk?"

He leaned over the saddle. "I've *been* riding. I have just ridden this bike for nearly three hours. I bike everywhere I go, as well as every day before work and on vacations too. Everyone," he added with a smile, "has some hidden vice if you look hard enough for it. Mine's exercise."

"The person I work for's is tenrecs," I informed him. I continued on my way, but at the crossing I glanced back. He was wiping his neck with the sleeve of his sweater. He flapped the cuff at me. He looked pretty human that way. But how, I wondered, could a grown man be afraid of dogs? Still, he was amazingly different from school. I wondered what would happen if he met Dr. Hogg with me and was swept off his feet. I wondered what he'd think of someone whose vice was clinging to dying animals for dear life.

At the Institute, Dr. Hogg was so wrapped up with her vice that even the slow loris was momentarily forgotten. It had to do with the tenrec's vital signs, which were undergoing a dramatic change right before her eyes. "I'm going to save this damn beastie," she muttered. One long, useful-looking finger stroked the coarse hairs along its back. I couldn't see any difference at all, but Dr. Hogg could. Her instruments could. "Where's that camera? Do you have it?"

I fished it out of my pocket and held it out to her.

She shook her head. "You do it. The way I showed you yesterday."

So I snapped a picture of the tenrec in her hand, and then I went off to Jerry.

He was no different. I was more tired and less patient. An hour later I went back to see what progress there was with the tenrec. Another person was there with a better camera. He took a picture. I went back to Jerry.

After another hopeless hour, I got a cold drink and ate my lunch. I stopped in on Dr. Hogg just in time to take another picture of her. She wasn't holding the tenrec anymore, but she was busy with something that took both hands. This time I couldn't wind the film in the camera. I tried as hard as I could, but it wouldn't budge.

"Never mind. Put the camera on my desk and I'll take it over to the darkroom later. Film's probably jammed. Go get Fred and ask him to bring his camera."

I nodded. I didn't dare tell her I had no idea who or where Fred was. "She wants Fred and his camera," I reported to the secretary. I went back to Jerry. My pocket felt empty.

Later when I was going down the hall to the ladies' room, Dr. Hogg came out of the lab. I guess I looked depressed or tired, because she told me not to worry about the camera, not to worry about the slow loris. I said I was sorry I'd made a mess of everything. I really did feel pretty low, and the thylacine didn't enter into it at all. He was like a dream. Maybe he was a dream. Maybe I'd made up all that about the Others too. Maybe Mr. Blanc was right and that I needed to learn how to tell the difference between reality and fantasy.

"I may spend the night here tonight," Dr. Hogg said to me. "How would you like to go home and get a sleeping bag and keep the vigil with me?"

I mumbled something about how that might be O.K. if my parents let me. She couldn't hear me, so I cleared my throat and tried to thank her. I couldn't even look at her. I didn't know anyone could be so sensitive as to consider a kid like me when her whole being was focused on a waking tenrec. I escaped into the bathroom and waited till the hall was clear.

I didn't go back to Jerry, though; I went to the zoo. I had to see for myself. If I found the Old Lion House not smelling of the Others, I would go to Mr. Blanc and confess everything and beg him to cure me. He'd probably prescribe hard exercise. I shuddered at the thought of three hours of bike riding every morning before school.

There was a funny atmosphere at the zoo. People seemed distracted, and the animals were restless and wary. The Old Lion House seemed shabbier now, not quite so overpowering. Still it had the look of a fortress, though along the side I saw outdoor cages with little trapdoors that probably connected with the indoor cages. Above them, in thick white brush strokes on the reddish stone, was painted: NO EXHIBITS. The whole place looked as though no one had gone near it for ages.

Nobody noticed me poking around there, so I felt pretty safe over on the far side. But as soon as I got within smelling distance, there was a sudden rush over my head. I saw a winged shadow zooming down. I ducked. A minute later, the shadow struck again. This time I plopped down on the steps and covered my head.

In that moment, when the wings were coming at me, so did the smell of that place, not like a dream, but sour and real. I dared to look up. A big brownish bird was swerving away from me and soaring after a tiny black and white bird that fluttered to safety through the bars of the outdoor cages. The little auk called to me: "Get away from there. That skua is guarding the Old Lion House. It'll keep after you till you go."

I scrambled down the steps. "W at about you?"

"Go on," he ordered. "I'll take care of myself."

So I started back toward the people part of the zoo, where a whole lot of visitors were intent on the sky instead of on the exhibits.

"Must be the airport," someone was saying in a loud voice. "The jets disorient the birds."

CHEETAH *Acinonyx Jubatus*

"It's this early spring," said another. "It's upset their schedule."

"But these aren't migrating," came another comment.

I didn't see the bird that had attacked me, but I could make out something big circling in the sky. Farther off, past the zoo wall, other large birds seemed to float over the treetops. And beyond them, beating up between tall buildings, still more birds went diving into distances and depths and out of sight.

At the cheetah's cage the brownish bird was just taking off again, but it didn't seem the least bit interested in me now. The cheetah was seated with its tail wrapped round like a royal robe. Because of all the excitement over the birds, no other person was there just then. Still, the cheetah isn't someone you just talk to when you feel like it. I stood and waited for it to notice me.

There was a shrill whistling overhead, and a huge bird with a terrible curving beak landed on top of the cheetah cage. "Sighted him," whistled the bird. "Followed him for miles. Two frozen streams, straight and very thin, run side by side along a flat river bed."

The cheetah eyed me. "Do you know what the eagle means? Where those streams are?"

I said I'd need more clues. I asked for descriptions. The eagle clenched and unclenched one talon, then spoke of drippings on a ledge where Thylacine had stopped to sniff, to taste. Listening to the eagle, I realized he was speaking of the city. I asked about the frozen streams, and this time he called them thin ridges of ice running at the bottom of a rock-hard gulley.

"Streetcar tracks," I exclaimed. "Or subway, or

train. Where did you lose him?" But the eagle wouldn't answer me. "Where did he lose sight of him?" I asked the cheetah.

The cheetah questioned the eagle, who replied that Thylacine had followed the ice streams down a steep slope and into the ground. "Tell the hen harrier," the cheetah said to the eagle. "Tell the sparrow hawk. Maybe they can go into the ground too."

Abruptly the eagle took off. He flapped heavily till he was away from us; then he spread his wings and climbed into the sky.

That was when he was noticed. People stood gaping. They spoke of his power, his grace.

The cheetah wrinkled its deep-lined face. "Late last night I myself followed Thylacine for a while. Till he entered a great cavern, something like what the eagle described, but no streams. I started in too, but there was a terrible roar. I couldn't go any farther without knowing what beast was in that lair. So I waited, hoping Thylacine might come out. Waited till it began to grow light and dangerous. I was still crouched at the cave mouth when the hen harrier found me and said she'd just seen Thylacine nearly run down by a thing that was larger than a rhinoceros. And faster and noisier."

"You mean a truck? It's a miracle Thylacine wasn't hit. You should let me tell Dr. Hogg right now. Can't you see you'll never catch Thylacine like this? Besides, everyone's looking at the birds."

"Not all the birds," the cheetah replied. "Many more are out searching than you or any other person will ever see."

"But you need a person who knows the city and can

get the right kind of help and equipment. Look, you'd have had no idea what those frozen streams were if I hadn't been here."

The cheetah gazed at me. "Come back tonight then. After dark."

I tried to push for Dr. Hogg too, but the cheetah wouldn't even hear me out. "No one. Nothing. Especially not the camera."

I opened my mouth to say that there was no chance I'd have the camera, when a whole flock of kids and grownups with baby carriages swarmed down on us. Quickly I turned and left.

On my way back to the Institute I stopped in on Benjamin, who wasn't attracting his usual attention as a small dinosaur exhibit because he was sleeping off last night's excitement.

"Wake up, Benjamin," I called softly. "Things are looking up."

"I'll say they are," muttered the little auk, who appeared suddenly in front of the python cage. "It's not a fit day out for little birds. Or," he added, cocking his head at me, "careless kids."

"Would that brown bird really have hurt me?"

"It or another. And most certainly killed me. Those skuas stun you with one whack of their wing, then tear you to bits."

"That's awful." I was feeling guilty because the little auk had had to lead the skua away from me. "They shouldn't be allowed out then. It's too dangerous."

"Yes," the little auk agreed, "I pity the small creatures in their way, but we need a day-shift on this thylacine hunt, and only the birds can get away in daylight. But you know how it is: those birds of prey don't stick by the rules; in that sense they're more like the Others than us. You know," he murmured, preening nervously, "a peregrine falcon nearly got me on my way over here."

"That's terrible," I blurted.

"Oh, I don't blame it. That's its nature. But as for you," he declared with his bright eye on me, "you can curb your curiosity. Stay away from the Old Lion House. We mustn't draw attention to it."

I said, "If you ask me, it's pretty big not to be noticeable."

"People usually stop seeing things they're not using. As long as nothing unusual happens, places like that are simply ignored till they're torn down. That's the way of people."

Benjamin, awake finally, said to me, "Why aren't you where Jerry is?"

"It's my lunch break. And I have to go home and get my sleeping bag." Even as I said this, I realized I couldn't be in two places at once tonight. How would I work it? My parents could think I was at the Institute. What would Dr. Hogg think? That I didn't care enough about the tenrec to keep the vigil with her?

I appealed to the little auk. "Couldn't you convince the cheetah that we need someone like Dr. Hogg, not only for finding and catching, but for keeping that thylacine from harming itself?"

"No person. It's the rule. Broken with you, and at what cost. No person. The Others managed till you interfered. They would have continued to manage."

"And when the zoo tears down that Old Lion

House?" Suddenly the little auk was really paying attention to me. "I know about thylacines. They need lots of space. Space is what Dr. Hogg can arrange for. Even if the Others get him back, they can't go on like this. Thylacine will want to roam. He'll be miserable. He must be miserable already, cooped up that way and confused."

"There's no way of telling what he feels," said the little auk. "He's never learned to speak with us."

"But he must show his feelings."

"He can't. He doesn't curl his lips or grin or flick his ears or even wag his tail. He just trots on and on until one of the Others leads him back to his den."

"That's a terrible existence. If Dr. Hogg—"

"At least he's alive. That is, if he isn't finished off by a dog or a truck or a person."

"But what good will it do? He's always alone."

"Maybe not forever. Other marsupials get shipped here from Tasmania once in a while."

"You mean you know there are more thylacines there?"

The little auk cocked his head. "How can I tell? I do get around, but I've never been that far. All I know right now is that I'm supposed to keep an eye out for you, which I've been doing, and for that picture you took."

"Oh, no," I blurted. "Dr. Hogg has the film. She took the camera. I tried to take a picture of the tenrec for her, because it may be an historic occasion. See, the tenrec's showing signs of waking up. Only it may die before it wakes enough to eat and drink, so Dr. Hogg's spending a lot of time with it because it's so slow."

"The picture," the little auk prompted.

"Yes, well, I tried to take.... Only the camera

jammed . . . and I tried. . . . Dr. Hogg said she could take care of it."

"Can you get it back?"

"She probably has to take out the film. She'll have it developed."

There was a long silence. A few visitors strolled by; they didn't notice the little auk; they didn't pay any attention to me. Benjamin was so still that he was easy to ignore too.

"You'll have to get it back," the little auk pronounced finally.

"How?"

"Use your imagination. And while you're at it, use it to figure out where Thylacine is likely to go."

"My imagination," I repeated gloomily.

"Yes," he said. "It's what you've got more of than anyone else I know."

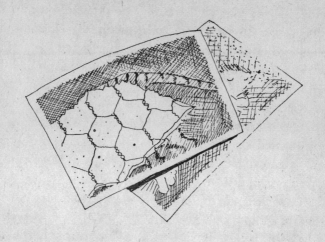

13 I got my sleeping bag and went back to the Institute. The afternoon stretched ahead of me like a century. After dropping my sleeping bag off in Dr. Hogg's outer office, I stopped in to see the tenrec. Dr. Hogg was still there. It was like one of those stories where the hero has a long adventure and then wakes up at home to find nothing changed. I had a sudden vision of being grown up, of doing the same thing day in and day out. Being a zoologist like Dr. Hogg meant being stuck here reading charts and noting boring metabolic changes in an animal that was probably dying. She never went anywhere exciting; she hardly stirred. If I were Dr. Hogg, I thought, I might get so desperate I'd take up biking three hours every morning before work.

"There's your camera." She beckoned with her head. "You've got fresh film."

I held my breath. She didn't add anything. I

squeezed my eyes shut waiting for the explosive shout: "There's a thylacine in your pictures!" Nothing, no shout. After a moment, Dr. Hogg murmured something.

I opened my eyes. "What?" I pretended to be busy with the camera.

"I said, you need to work on your focusing."

Then I saw the pictures lying on a pad. The one on top showed Dr. Hogg's fingers all out of proportion and only a part of the tenrec. "Are these all that came out?" I asked, picking them up.

"Don't be disappointed. It was your first try. One of them is quite nice."

With my back to her, I riffled through the few pictures. My hands were shaking so hard I dropped the lot and had to scramble all over the floor after them. She kicked one out from under the table. A single quick glance showed me something that looked like a blurry rope in the photograph. There were faint, regular markings across the rope thing.

I took the picture to the light. My hands weren't shaking anymore, but I could feel my heart pounding and I was afraid to let Dr. Hogg see my face. I stared at Thylacine's tail. No other part of him showed. And over all the gray and black was a fuzzy honeycomb pattern that mystified me, till suddenly I remembered that thick glass with the chicken wire in it. Then I realized that not only had Thylacine bounded away while I was taking his picture, but that I had still been holding that glass out in front when I aimed the camera at him.

"You'll learn," said Dr. Hogg. "It takes practice."

I slipped the picture into my pocket. I left the rest on the table. But as I opened the door, she turned, and she looked so discouraged and worn that I couldn't bear the secret I was carrying away with me. "I made it up," I blurted. "About the Tasmanian Tiger. Thylacine. About sources I couldn't divulge."

Either she was more exhausted than I'd realized or she wasn't especially surprised.

"I made it all up." I was nearly shouting at her.

She nodded.

The picture in my pocket felt heavier than the gloves and camera put together. "Not about the slow loris, though. That was true."

She nodded again.

I couldn't bear it. Now that I was confessing, I was concealing even more. Somewhere out there a poor terrified thylacine, a real live one, was lost and in danger. I had set it off. I was powerless to save it. And Dr. Hogg, who might know what to do, could not be told. Whatever I did or didn't do would be a betrayal of someone. And I was in this mess because I had let my imagination go.

Use your imagination, the little auk had told me. But when I used it, it got me into trouble, just the way Mr. Blanc predicted. *Use your imagination to get us out of this jam,* the little auk had asked of me.

"I imagine things sometimes," I said, then stumbled to a halt. Dr. Hogg was still nodding, but she had that scowl which meant that something intense was going on inside her head. "I imagined about the thylacine." *Use your imagination.* "What if," I began, trying to keep my voice level, "what if there was such a thing like what I put in my report and the Beast...the thylacine got away? Where do you suppose—I mean, just imagining— it would go?"

She had to turn back to that tenrec of hers. She jotted something down on her graph. She was still bent over her things when she spoke. "There was a certain species of wolf that lived on the Falkland Islands and nowhere else. When the islands were first settled, the wolves had no fear of the people." She straightened, but kept looking down at the tenrec. "An ideal situation for collecting data about how the species passed on survival information. The settlers discovered with little trouble that both wolf parents cared for the young and taught them to hunt. So now we have that information. But we

don't have the Falkland Island wolves." Her eyes met mine. "The settlers also found that they could hold out meat in one hand and kill the wolves with the other. Not one survived."

I couldn't free myself from her look. Everything she felt about that massacre strained toward me, and I knew that she wasn't just delivering a lecture on an extinct wolf.

She kept on talking. She said there were other animals that were easily tamed, but changed or whose young changed in confinement. She said that we were just beginning to learn the drastic effects of what might appear to be trivial alterations of environment on species whose survival hangs in the balance. She said that some animals, when released, seek only what they know.

She was still looking at me that way, speaking as much with her eyes as with her words, so that it took a while for what she meant to sink in. And I got the queerest feeling that at this very moment she believed there really was something about a thylacine that I wasn't telling her. "And if it were true," she went on in such a low voice that I could hardly hear her, "even if there was a lost thylacine, that would be a wonderful thing to know, because it would mean the species wasn't extinct. Because there is always hope that what is lost may be found. The knowledge of one lost thylacine would be like a present. But if the only chance to save it was wasted, that would be terrible."

The words echoed in my mind: *wonderful, hope, terrible.* I said, "When I started out with 'The Beast on the Brink,' I didn't know I was making up anything . . . important. I didn't think it could hurt."

"And now?" she said softly.

And now it was worse. I knew exactly what I was doing. "And now...." I couldn't go on. There was nowhere to go, except that I had to get away from her sight. Talk about special membranes and feeling things in your bones. Dr. Hogg seemed to have more ways of telling what was going on than any animal I knew of. I felt that now I truly grasped the cheetah's need for distance; I understood why some animals couldn't survive crowding. Dr. Hogg stood there, never moving, but closing in on me with her mind, and I could hardly breathe. "And now...." I groped for the door handle behind me. "Now I'd better get back to the slow loris and see what can be done."

Dr. Hogg's eyes let go of me. She said, "If he's still withdrawn by the end of the day, we may have to resort to a stimulant. We don't need another inert animal around here. I suspect," she added, "that if we checked, we'd find his temperature has dropped too. Not a good sign." And with this comment, she turned back to her work.

I don't know whether it was what she said or just everything mounting up, but the Observation Room seemed about the gloomiest place in the world. Jerry still hadn't budged. I sat and watched him not move. I thought about the tenrec and how its temperature had dropped during estivation and how probably Jerry's temperature was dropping too. What if he never woke up again?

All of a sudden I wanted to feel him to see if he was cold. And get him to feel me. Maybe if I rubbed him hard and breathed on his face and hands he would warm up and come awake. I unfastened the cage door, which swung out heavily. I pulled everything out of my pockets but the picture, in order to cram myself through that opening. I couldn't fit both shoulders through, but I got my head in there and one hand, which I reached up to Jerry. He was colder than he should have been, so I stroked him and stroked him.

Then I had to shift my position. I tipped my head sideways. It was awkward, because I couldn't see him at all. I found that I was facing a kind of smeary picture of myself in the open cage door. I stared, then I let go of Jerry and wriggled out of there. I shut the door and looked through it. There was Jerry. I opened the door and looked at Jerry's side of it. There I was, with blurry squiggles across my face.

I was so excited I jumped up and down. "Don't you see?" I yelled at Jerry. "It's a one-way window. For observing animals. Oh, Jerry, you're not blind. Nothing's wrong. Jerry, wake up now. Please."

But he was in that deep cold sleep, and I guess it took time and also something more to bring him out of it. *Use your imagination.* I got busy with the idea of reversing the cage door to prove to Jerry that he was fine. I lifted it off those things it swings on and managed to turn it around, but then I was stuck. "Oh, help," I grunted. "I need at least two more hands." Of course I was talking to myself. The special glass in the door made it heavy, and it was too wide to ease into place by myself. I struggled, though, because I didn't dare let go, and then all at once the weight lightened. Jerry's hands, with their amazing fingers, took over the balancing, and in no time we had the door in place and sliding down, till it hung free, back to front. It shut perfectly.

I stared in through the glass at my weird double. I opened the door, and there sat Jerry facing me, his eyes wide, his arms stretched out. I showed him how the one-way window worked. He sat on my shoulder and made faces at himself in the swirly mirror.

"See?" I pointed out. "No one can tell whether there's anything in that cage or not."

Then we both looked at each other. Without another word, Jerry let himself down into the deep pocket of my lab coat. Firmly, quietly, I shut the door of the cage and fastened the catch securely. Unless I walked around to the side, I'd have no idea that the cage was empty.

There was nothing more to do now, except wait. I reached down. A small pair of hands took hold of my middle finger. The small hands were warm and gentle to the touch.

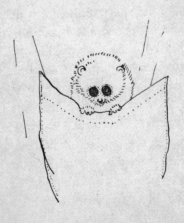

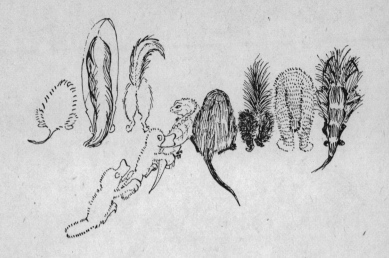

14 I couldn't wait till dark. As soon as I saw the last of the keepers leaving the zoo, I slithered under the wall. Animals were already beginning to gather in small clusters. I saw Ernest nervously tugging Winifred back from the biggest group; she seemed about to be swallowed up in the press of legs and tails. Then I realized that Benjamin's tail was showing. Ernest hauled on Winifred, and Winifred dragged Benjamin backwards with her.

I decided to surprise them. I dashed from tree to building to tree until I was on the downhill side of the crowd. The cheetah was at its center, stretched full length on a concrete bench. I listened from behind the tree. Jerry chittered at me and I patted his head. "We'll surprise them," I said.

"But it's   Others."

"I know. It must be safe, though. This is a special occasion."

The cheetah was fending off the Others, all of them clamoring for recognition. Why had the common animals been allowed to search? the fossa demanded. Why the dingo? Why the wolverine?

Before the cheetah could answer, the raccoon dog was growling that Thylacine would run from any ordinary animal, as he would from a dog or a cat.

The cheetah moaned. "Your time is coming. With the night. Only a few animals were sent to run the twilight hours, and only the hunters that hunt alone, whose ways are closest to Thylacine's."

"And if they catch up with him?" asked the small-eared dog. "What good will it do?"

The cheetah gave a bony shrug. "The girl may have an idea."

"The girl," rumbled the hog-badger, "is the cause of all this. Why listen to her?"

From somewhere in the midst of the crowd an animal hissed, "She'sss ressssponsssible for the haunting of the SSSmall Animal Housssse too. Who needsss her?"

Benjamin escaped from Winifred's clutches and pressed forward. "Oh, but wait." No one made room for him.

"The girl's no hunter," whined the bush dog. "It's a mistake to rely on her."

Benjamin kept trying. "About the haunting, there's something you ought to know."

"I have the distinction," declared the aardwolf, shouting Benjamin down, "of being the only one of the Others who isn't, in the strictest sense, a hunter, and I can assure you all—"

"Please, someone, listen to me," pleaded Benjamin. "I'm talking about haunting, not hunting."

"Benjamin," called Winifred. "Come back. Over here." She and Ernest had worked their way downhill and were standing midway between the crowd and me, as Benjamin was squeezed back toward them.

"It's a risk," the cheetah was saying, "but the girl is changing...."

I wish I could have heard the rest of what the cheetah had to say about me, but Winifred interfered. She had her webbed paws wrapped around Benjamin's spiny middle and she was scolding him. "You can't just move in like that with all those Others. Never mind what the numbat's up to; it isn't in its right mind. How long do you think you'd last in there?"

"But somebody has to clear up the mistake about the haunting."

"Never mind haunting, Benjamin. Do you know what Tasmanian devils and thylacines can't resist? Morsels like you, Benjamin. And us."

Benjamin's points stood straight up. "Us? Me? But how do you know?"

"They don't just eat wallabies," Ernest explained. "They eat all sorts of lizards too. Now Thylacine, wherever he is, must be famished. As for the devil, she's always unpredictable."

"But last night," Benjamin stammered, "last night, last night. . . ."

"Last night," said Winifred with a sniff, "you risked your life to keep Lena company."

Benjamin's points rattled like chattering teeth.

I couldn't stay hidden. Benjamin was terrified, and Winifred was making it sound like all my fault. I made my appearance with my hands in my pockets, striding like Dr. Hogg and being commanding. "Stop scaring Benjamin," I told her. "The cheetah wouldn't have let anything bad happen to him."

"It wouldn't have let anything bad happen to Thylacine either," Winifred retorted, "if it could have helped it."

We glared at each other. I felt terrible. Winifred sounded practically like my enemy now.

She poked her duckbill toward the bulge in my pocket. "Gloves?" she taunted. "Camera?"

I couldn't help grinning as I plunged my hand deep into the pocket and felt Jerry twine himself around my wrist. Then he was out, clinging to me, but waving one elastic arm at his friends.

"Jerry," cried Winifred, "you're all right!"

Benjamin said, "Lena told us he was going to be all right."

Winifred darted a glance at me that was almost friendly. "Did you steal him?"

"Borrowed."

"What if Dr. Hogg finds out?" Ernest asked anxiously.

"Right now she's too busy to notice. She's staying with the tenrec tonight."

"Besides," chittered Jerry, "even if   never know   . Can't see in."

Winifred spoke to me in the old, easy way. "What does he mean?"

So I told them, with Jerry helping, about the queer door that you could only see through one way.

Winifred clapped her paws to her eyes. "Like a giant mask. Poor Jerry. No one likes to be seen like that."

"I don't know," Ernest considered. "If you've got nothing to hide. . . ."

Winifred cut him off. "Some animals are more sensitive than others. I don't blame Jerry for going to sleep to hide. I'd feel the same way. I'd hate it if our water was clear everywhere without any mud for being private."

Benjamin asked Jerry if he was on his way back to the Small Animal House.

"And miss   excite   ment?"

Winifred giggled. "You really are all right then, aren't you."

"I'm with Lena," Jerry answered simply, and for one

blissful moment we were all really with each other just like that, and we nearly forgot we were in the middle of a crisis.

The feeling couldn't last, though. The raccoon dog was already trotting over to tell us that the cheetah was waiting.

Brave Benjamin led the way, and this time the animals parted for him. Winifred snuffled. "Smells like the devil around here," she muttered.

"Devil's gone," the raccoon dog informed her.

Winifred let out a little sigh. "It's nerve-wracking being so close."

"I know what you mean," the raccoon dog agreed. "I remember at the start how unnerving that devil could be. Never knew whether she was going to nurse the thylacine baby or gobble it up."

"The devil's gone off to collect herself," the cheetah declared. "She's not much use when she's this frantic, and I'm sure we'll need her before we're through." The cheetah looked at me. "Now, girl, Thylacine's been sighted again. We thought he might be on his way back here, but he keeps dashing in and out of those dark caves and pits."

"He'll be run over," whined the bush dog. "He's tiring. The wolverine saw him bumping into things."

"I think he is trying to come home," I told them. "You'd better be there when he does."

"But where? We've tried every sort of home. Last night we spread out to cover all the places that could possibly resemble real thylacine country."

"The rocky ledges in the park," snorted the hog-badger.

"The thorn bushes around the great buildings," whimpered the small-eared dog.

"The crumbly ditches at the bottom of a ravine," rasped the fossa.

"The great plain of dead trucks, which is so impenetrable only a thylacine could make its way over the treacherous rubble."

"Dead trucks?" Winifred's voice was hushed with awe. "Doesn't something eat them when they die? Just think of all those old truck bodies piled up."

Later on, I thought, I'd try to reassure her about junk yards and scrap metal, but right now I had to deal with the Others. "All Thylacine knows," I explained, "is the Old Lion House."

"Not the plains? Not the ravine? Not—"

"All he knows is this zoo and his secret den underneath—"

"Below. In the ground." The cheetah switched its tail. "Down the steps and way beneath us."

I nodded. "The subway. And there are lots of entrances. You never saw him come up last night because they all connect."

"We'll need many animals then. All kinds."

Jerry peeped out of my big pocket. "Let me. My hands."

The cheetah regarded the eager eyes banded with dark fur, the hand with its long, supple fingers.

"What about the potto?" I suggested. "You never know when an extra hand will come in handy. I found that out."

"Won't come," Jerry predicted.

"At the Institute they stick a pole in the cage and

gently prod the stubborn primates, which then usually grab hold. They're carried that way."

"We don't have a pole."

"What potto?" cried a chorus of voices.

"In my   cage," said Jerry. "Instead   me."

"But it'sss a ghossst," hissed the numbat.

"I don't think   so," Jerry responded. "Anyhow, not mine   ."

"If you'd looked carefully," I added, "you'd have seen its bit of tail. You all just assumed it was exactly like Jerry. But its color's different. Also, it has things on the back of its neck like bones."

"Ssso what if it never uncurled? How could we tell any of that?" The numbat lumbered away, then turned back for a moment. "Whatever it isss, I wisssh you would take it with you. It'sss keeping usss all awake with itsss ghossstly ssshrieks. Imposssible sssituation."

"Do you know whether your keeper has a pole?" I called to it.

"Get one of the hoofed animalsss with long hornsss," suggested the numbat. "The gemsbok ought to be able to reach it." And the numbat hurried on to spread the news to all the other small animals that their building wasn't haunted after all, that a living something called a potto was a temporary resident there.

"Get some antelope that won't be afraid of me," the cheetah ordered.

No one stirred.

"Well, get the oryx then. The Arabian oryx. It's so close to extinction itself it can't refuse to help a threatened fellow."

124

At this, the raccoon dog trotted off, and the rest of us trouped after the cheetah. By the hole under the wall, it told the Others to wait on the zoo side. The fossa could alert the aardvark to close up the hole.

"There's a subway map somewhere around here," I told the cheetah, as we all gathered again on the other side of the wall. "It tells you how to get to the zoo, or away from it." I found the map on a great big board bolted to the zoo wall where it faced the street that led to the subway. There was an arrow on it with a star at the end. "You are here," said some badly scratched print next to the arrow. I studied the map for a long time, but it didn't seem to have any relation to what I saw around me.

"Well?" said the cheetah.

"It's getting too dark. I can hardly read it. You'd think they're put it under a street light."

"I suppose," offered Winifred, "they don't expect many night visitors."

I glanced down at her, ready to be sarcastic, but she was just a small furry blob sticking very close to another one, which was Ernest, and I got the feeling she was trying hard to sound normal so no one would realize how scared she was.

I showed the cheetah where we were. I made everyone turn around to face uphill, but then I had to face uphill too, and as soon as my back was to the map I forgot everything I was supposed to be showing them. I turned again and peered at the map. "Now that way," I said aloud, just to fix it in my own mind, "is uptown. . . ." I pointed with my right hand.

The cheetah said, "It's getting late. Can't you simply tell us where to block Thylacine if he does go into the ground?"

I stared and stared at the subway map. I put one finger at one blue square, another finger at another. "More fingers," I called, and Jerry crept out onto my shoulder. "There," I told him. "And there."

"Is it all right if we turn around?" said the cheetah as it joined me to peer at the map. My hands felt glued to the board. Jerry, reaching above me, pressed his long fingers to other spots.

"Do you see?" I stretched with all my might. "These are exits that say, NO ENTRANCE AFTER MID-NIGHT. That means the people with change lock up their cages and go away."

"Cages?" growled the cheetah. "Is that what you think Thylacine is looking for?"

"I don't know enough about what he's used to. Either cages or a dark, dank underground place. What he knows and feels safe in." I stepped back and let my hands relax, leaving Jerry hanging by his feet on the sign. "After midnight you can get the animals stationed at those spots. But they'd better be careful. People can still get off the subway there. Not," I added, looking around at the empty street, "that many are likely to come here."

We waited uneasily. From time to time the cheetah called to an animal in birdlike chirps that didn't seem to match its tense, graceful power. One after another, the animals were shown the subway stops, but as none of them knew how to read maps, the night birds had to show them where to go. Jerry was the pointer. I couldn't see the map at all anymore, but the owls and nightjars had no trouble seeing where Jerry pointed. Meanwhile, the two platypuses and the tuatara kept out of the way. I almost forgot they were there huddled against the wall.

Some of the animals returned to report that they had glimpsed Thylacine. The dingo came rubbing his face frantically against his forepaws, on the sidewalk, even against the cheetah's flank. "A hunter," he panted. "Nearly got Thylacine."

Everyone went still. The dingo flung himself down and rolled, pawing his eyes. "At first," he whimpered "I thought it was a collision. I was tracking Thylacine, dodging into doorways, weaving through alleys and out into empty streets. And suddenly, as he turned onto a big street, he was run into. Or maybe it was the other way around. He's been bumping into things a lot. Anyway, I couldn't tell, because I was staying back to keep from alarming him. He met a man on wheels. I don't think he knew what hit him. He must have been stunned. But the man wasn't. I saw him draw a gun, and I hurled myself between Thylacine and the hunter. So the hunter aimed his gun at me instead, and Thylacine got away."

"Are you hurt?" asked the cheetah.

"I don't know what he shot me with. It burned my eyes. It was terrible then. Now it just feels like bee stings."

"Could you show the bush dog where you were shot? Where you lost Thylacine?"

The dingo, still rubbing his eyes desperately, agreed to take the bush dog there and then return.

By now it was past midnight. I was anxious to get going, but the cheetah was sending out animals, calling in birds, warily biding its time. "Where's that oryx?" it demanded, and a small animal I could barely see scrambled under the wall and scurried off into the darkness.

Waiting like this seemed to me as bad as waiting for the tenrec to wake up. I needed to do something. "What about making the hole big enough for the oryx?" I suggested.

Before the cheetah could respond, the oryx came streaking toward us with something dangling from one of its elegant horns. The oryx cleared the wall as if it were flying. It landed just beyond us and gathered itself to

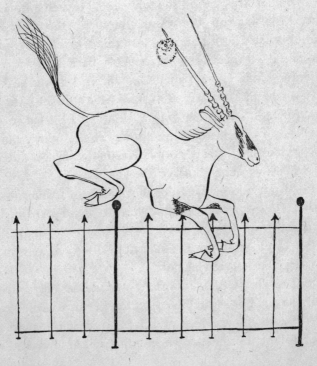

charge forward. The potto, dangling upside-down from its horn, shrilled its nonstop protest, goading the poor oryx on. We started after it, till Jerry called from the sign. I went back to pick him up, but he insisted on riding on the other oryx horn so that he could calm down the furious potto.

"All right, potto," Jerry soothed. "All right, oryx."

"Don't call me potto," screamed the little animal. The great delicate oryx shuddered. "I'm a particular potto. I'm Softly Softly."

I reached up with Jerry and set him on the empty horn. The oryx flared its nostrils; its neck quivered.

"Use the night voice," growled the cheetah. "Softly."

"No," shrieked the potto. "Two ones. Softly Softly."

The oryx flinched, but held still. The cheetah stalked ahead. I felt a small tug at my ankle. Winifred was there asking if my pockets were empty. I scooped the platypuses up and plopped them into my pockets. Then I ran to catch up with the cheetah.

Benjamin tried to follow, glancing at everything around him with bewilderment. Except for a few parked cars and a bunch of trash cans and something else rolled in plastic and lying in the gutter, the street was empty. A shred of the plastic scratched at itself like something alive. Benjamin eyed it; he watched the cheetah stride past it.

The cheetah headed toward a street with two levels, an upper one like a bridge, and a dark underpass with heavy support columns. I don't think Benjamin even saw that far. He swung his heavy head from side to side, staring at the continuous line of buildings that faced each other across the street. He stopped to look back at the zoo wall. "I hope I don't forget where that hole is," he mumbled, then jerked back suddenly as the plastic scraped extra hard against the curb.

I stopped to lift him up, draping his cool dry body over my arm. With relief he looked down into a pocket out of which one duckbill poked. "Ernest?" he whispered. "Where's Winifred?"

"In the other pocket."

Benjamin twisted around for a look at her, his points tickling and making me yelp.

"Oh, sorry." His voice was muffled by the creases of my too-big sleeve.

I said I was sorry too. I said the last thing I wanted to sound like was that awful potto.

And then I realized that the potto had shut up. All I could hear now were the sharp hoof treads of the oryx and Jerry's slow, quiet chittering. As Jerry recited to the potto the plight of the Beast on the Brink, our small procession worked its way toward the underpass where a light at the corner showed the stairwell to the subway.

TRAVEL

You've seen them in the zoo. Now experience them in their natural state.

Inquire about our BARGAIN SAFARI

15 Before we reached the stairwell, two couples appeared out of the subway opening and turned down the hill toward us. The cheetah froze. I glanced around. Most of the buildings we'd passed were stores and businesses. One of these just ahead had a kind of alcove backed by glass and a large window front advertising exotic tours. "Quick," I whispered. "In here." *You've seen them in the zoo,* ran the message over the poster showing a giraffe; *Now experience them in their natural state. Inquire about our bargain safari!* "Closer," I directed, as the oryx hung back. "Lie down, Cheetah. Make room." I squatted down behind the oryx.

We could hear the couples coming closer, their voices full of laughter.

"Some short cut," ran one woman's voice. "I knew we should've gotten out at the next stop."

"But look at what you get to see. Look at that travel agency. Some display, huh?"

"I don't know. They overdo these things. Like those monkeys on the antelope horns. It's too much."

They started to move on, but the sound of hard panting made one of the men turn around. "Hey, it's a dog. Let's see what he makes of those stuffed animals." The couples stood watching as the tawny dingo charged up to the alcove, stopped, and faced the motionless cheetah. The cheetah gave one low chirp. The dingo got the message. He stiffened, his hackles rising, and stepped back.

"Now there's an argument against that kind of display," the other man remarked with a laugh. "All the stray dogs in town will want to test those things."

"I'd think there's a worse danger. Having them stolen."

"Stolen?" The man laughed again. "What are you going to do with a stuffed leopard at two o'clock in the morning?" He held out his hand, advancing and still laughing. "Here, boy, don't let those dummies get to you." The dingo's tail drooped; its head lowered.

"Don't touch that hound," advised his friend. "You never know what they've been into."

The couples lingered a moment longer before going on their way. We didn't move. Then, off in the distance, a baying came to us. The dingo whimpered.

The cheetah rose. "What is it?"

"They're after him."

"Hunters?"

"No, a dog pack. After I left the bush dog, I picked up Thylacine's scent. I didn't pay any attention at first when three dogs joined me. I was concentrating on Thylacine. We were so close. But after a while I realized it wasn't just three anymore. I was running with a pack. And they're still coming, all kinds. Last thing I saw, Thylacine was up there." The dingo raised his muzzle toward the overpass.

By now the howling pack had split at the ramp. One group streamed down below. And there, out of the stand of supporting columns, a striped wolflike body wheeled and sprang, spitting and wheezing at its attackers. As the dogs closed in, Thylacine reared up onto his hind legs and hurtled right through them.

The cheetah was a blur of speed. It met the other half of the pack full tilt at the corner. High above them, windows were shoved open. People shouted down to the street and one of them flung something at the dogs. The cheetah wheeled and, with a tremendous stamp of its forepaws, scattered the dogs.

Thylacine reappeared, this time loping clumsily right toward us. Then he saw us and shifted his ungainly body. He glanced back at the remnants of the pack, coughed, and caught sight of the hole at the corner of the street.

A moment after he'd bounded down into it, the cheetah started after him. I raced to the subway entrance. I heard the rumble of a distant train; the sound swelled and filled the blackness below. The cheetah emerged, growling. "I saw something. No face, only a single eye. I didn't see Thylacine."

There was a fluttering of wings as the little auk landed beside us. "Hard work, distracting people, keeping them from looking too closely."

"How can you do that?" Benjamin wanted to know.

"I have my ways." The little auk lifted his tail pointedly. "I fly overhead, take aim, and. . . ."

The cheetah was staring down the subway steps. "It's like no other place," it murmured. "There are things like gates and cages, a terrible edge over a pit. Where the roaring came from, the huge eye."

"You were right not to go after him," I said. "You could have driven him right off the platform, over the brink."

"We need someone small to go down," the little auk decided. "Someone who won't frighten Thylacine if they locate him. Maybe I should try."

"You can't see dark," said Jerry.

"That's true. I'm afraid it'll have to be you." The auk was poised to take flight. "And while you're locating Thylacine down there, I'll go get the devil. We'll need her here to deal with him."

"No," I shouted as the little auk flew up. "Jerry can't do that. Thylacines were voracious hunters. I mean, this one doesn't understand our rules. And Jerry's so small. And. . . ."

Benjamin squirmed to raise himself up from my arm. He had that look of concentration that reptiles sometimes get when they are about to pounce on something. "It's too bad Jerry doesn't have those spiny things on his neck like the potto," Benjamin remarked.

We all turned to look at the potto.

"Then," continued Benjamin, "if Thylacine tried to eat Jerry, Jerry could roll up and be prickly instead of soft."

We turned away from the potto and gazed at the furry loris.

"It's just too bad," Benjamin went on, "that Jerry doesn't have spurs on his neck to protect him. But it can't be helped."

"It's all right," Jerry assured us.

"No, it isn't," I snapped. "It's wrong. Why can't the potto go instead?"

The potto retorted, "The loris can roll up so tight that maybe Thylacine will think it's a potto and not try to eat it."

Jerry obligingly started to curl.

Benjamin raised himself still higher, until he was nearly level with the potto. "Softly Softly," said Benjamin, "can you see me?"

"Of course I can. And I know why you're calling me Softly Softly. You want to appeal to my better self."

Benjamin beamed at him as only a toothy tuatara can do. "You're amazing," he told the potto. "You not only have those hands and feet that can hold onto anything, you not only have that gorgeous fur and that magnificent voice and those hard little shields on the back of your neck, but you must also have some very special sensory membrane like my almost pineal eye, because you practically read my mind."

The potto eyed him suspiciously. "What are you getting at?"

Jerry peeked out from under his arm. "Is someone going to roll me?"

"Yes," I said. "Down the stair rail. It certainly is wonderful of you to do this to help the poor terrified thylacine." I deliberately left out *voracious*.

"What are you and Benjamin doing?" demanded Winifred in a loud whisper.

"Sssh," I warned her.

The potto waved his long sinuous arm. "No. Me first. Roll *me*." And he started to curl too.

"Get on with it," growled the cheetah.

"Terrific," Benjamin chuckled. "Softly Softly, you're going to be a hero."

"What about Jerry?" piped up Winifred. "Jerry was willing without any urging, without protection or—"

I cut her short with a glare. Benjamin winked at her.

"Oops," she whispered. "Sorry."

Then I set Jerry back on the oryx horn and took the furry potto in my hands. Setting him on the railing, I gave him a gentle shove. The neck spurs worked like treads, slowing his descent.

Benjamin got down on the step and stretched as far as he could, craning after the potto, which vanished into the darkness. "His better self," murmured the tuatara.

"You did that, Benjamin," Winifred told him. "You made it come true."

"No," said Benjamin. "Jerry set the example. Lena and I just did the shoving." He grinned at the little

136

platypus, who was on the verge of climbing out to join him until she caught sight of the dingo, its tongue still lolling. The dingo peered over my shoulder into the gloom. Winifred sank deep into my pocket.

There was a brief silence. The dingo bent to rub its eyes. The cheetah, looking guarded, held itself aloof, tense.

I whispered anxiously up to Jerry, "Are you sure the potto understands? Did you really explain everything to him before?"

"Help!" screamed a voice from below. Another faint roar began to swell in the darkness, but the potto's cry pierced the rumbling. "I have its tail. Help!"

I nearly trampled Benjamin. I scooped him up and was already on my way down when Jerry called from his perch on the oryx horn. The oryx spread its front legs and lowered its graceful neck until the horns dipped down to me. Foot over hand and hand over foot, Jerry inched along the slim horn to my shoulder. There he clung, and down we all went.

Benjamin gripped my arm. I don't know whether all the tiles made him think of the Old Lion House or whether he was frightened by the shreds of color plastering the wall. I felt him squirm at the sight of a gigantic hand holding a bottle, and cower as we passed a huge chalky smile with perfect teeth. Gashes and scrawls overlay all the posters; one of those perfect white teeth was blackened. I couldn't explain to him why this vast cavern, with its dim, soot-filmed lights, looked like this. I could only hug him to me and keep going.

Jerry was in a much better position. From my shoulder he could look past the picture of a tower and

137

through the cold, dismal space to the barricade and the tall round cage of the turnstyle. Behind that cage more stairs dropped into a lower darkness and beyond it other stairs led up again to the street. But we didn't have to look beyond the barricade, because Thylacine was right there, stuck so tightly that he was forced to stand upright. He was pressing against the narrow, confining gate. Behind him his tail stuck out through the bars, and attached to it, its adhesive feet gripping the iron railing behind, stretched one flat-out potto.

Benjamin finally saw all this and asked, "But how will we ever get him out of there?"

"Get him out," screamed the potto. "Then what am I holding him for?"

"Don't let go," I called. I started down the remaining steps. "And don't worry. A thylacine's tail doesn't bend. As long as you've got it, he can't turn on you."

"But he's trapped," Winifred cried out. "He can't move."

"He could if the potto lets go. That's a revolving door. A one-way gate."

"Like my cage?" chittered Jerry."

"No, not for looking. For passing through. Once you're in it you can't go backward."

"Well, this beast is going to go forward any minute," wailed the potto, "if I don't get some help here."

Thylacine tried to twist around, but the potto's grip on his rigid tail prevented him from turning. He showed neither terror nor rage, but his gaping jaws clamped onto the cold metal, and he snapped again and again with a terrible despair. Lifting his shoulder, he wedged one

138

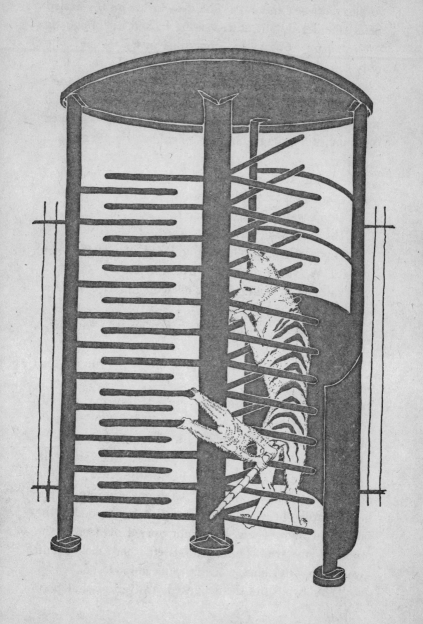

foreleg between the bars. The eyes in his dull, grizzled head smoldered, but otherwise he looked as though he was wearing a mask that concealed every feeling. The only sound he made was a hoarse, choking bark.

Jerry clambered up the railing, skirted Thylacine's paw, and moved, one limb at a time, all the way around until he was opposite the potto. There, he too clamped onto the tail, so that Thylacine couldn't budge an inch either way.

I stared at the trapped beast. How could such a young animal look so old, so used?

"Don't watch," Jerry called to me. "Not fair."

"He can't bear us," I whispered.

"If you ask me," Winifred declared, "He ought to be grateful. We've all risked our lives for him."

I said, "You can't expect Thylacine to be like the rest of us."

"He should have one-way window," Jerry said.

I nodded. "Miles and miles of one-way window. His way round."

From the top of the opposite stairway the cheetah growled a warning. At the same time, the distant rumbling vibrated through the underground floor.

"Where?" A grating voice filled the stairwell. "Where is he?" The smell of her drifting over us, the devil came lumbering down. After one glimpse of her heavy, ratlike head, Winifred and Ernest plopped to the bottom of my pockets. Benjamin buried his face in the crook of my arm. The devil hissed, then clicked and growled at Thylacine, whose gaping jaws closed.

"You two," the devil barked, "let go of that poor

tail." She coughed in the Other language. Thylacine didn't move. "What have you done to him?" the devil accused. "He's all muddled."

Together the slow loris and the potto climbed to the top of the gate's frame. Jerry stretched backward, pushing his legs through and pumping. The potto hung by his toes and prodded the bars of the inner structure. The gate began to revolve. As soon as it had moved out of range, he turned a slow-motion somersault that set him forward and ready to push some more. Meanwhile Jerry seemed to flow straight out till his legs could reach no farther. Thylacine had to shuffle forward on his hind legs. Jerry and the potto grunted with the effort of moving both gate and beast. Even when the bars meshed and Thylacine faced the opening, he just stood where he was as if he couldn't trust what he saw.

The devil wheezed and clicked. I could tell that all those angry, ugly sounds were beginning to get through to Thylacine. Still upright, he tilted forward. Then he staggered, blinked, and landed heavily on all four feet. He swung his head like a dog about to shake itself, cast one quick look up at the two furry creatures on top of the gate, and shuffled to the opposite stairway.

"Now he's off again," the devil snarled, her mouth enormously wide and pink, her teeth really frightening. "Because of you."

She lumbered down and across to the other side. "Wait," she called to him. "You've had me worried to death. You'll break my heart." She hissed back at me, "You see? You've even got me mixed up. Here I am talking to him in a language he can't understand." Her little eyes glittered; she broke into clicks and coughs.

"Don't worry," I told her. "Cheetah's there with him."

She struggled up the steps like a furry black pig, short in the legs and too heavy for them. "Wait, my cub, my little pup. Oh," she wheezed, "what a burden. It's too much. How could this have happened to me? Cheetah," she grunted, "wait for me."

As she disappeared sobbing, the two platypus duckbills emerged from my pockets, followed by two wide-eyed platypus faces.

"Are Tasmanian devils endangered too?" asked Benjamin.

"No such luck," said Ernest.

"You shouldn't speak like that," Benjamin told him. "Every creature has its place."

Winifred leaned her webbed paws over the top of the pocket and watched the potto and loris picking their way toward us. "That's all very well for you to say," she said to Benjamin, "but where we come from those devils happen to be the death of us. Besides," she added, "I bet

Aunt Martha would never admit any of those Others have a place around here."

The rumbling from down below was a dull roar now. Jerry latched onto my sleeve and crept to my shoulder. "What about me?" screeched the potto, grasping at my lab coat.

"All right," I said, still cradling Benjamin in my arms and hitching the potto onto my other shoulder, "as far as I'm concerned every animal has its place." Climbing the stairs was something of a balancing act. "Talk about burdens," I muttered to myself and heard an answering giggle from my pocket.

The cheetah met us at the top. "Thylacine's gone back. Flanked by all the Others. I sent the oryx and dingo along too." The cheetah's look was strained, as if it could just barely stand us anymore, but it allowed the loris and potto to ride on its tail as far as the zoo wall. Anything, it seemed to be telling us, to be done and rid of the lot of us.

I couldn't help asking, "What will happen to Thylacine now? Will he be safe?"

The cheetah shrugged its bony shoulders. "Only for as long as we remain alert. And together."

"What about after they tear down the Old Lion House?" I knew the cheetah hated questions, but I sensed this was my last chance to learn where and how Thylacine might be hidden.

The cheetah's eyes smoldered. "Who can tell what lies ahead for any of us? This hunt is over, and now comes the long sleep. And while we sleep, some must watch for us."

144

I could feel its eyes burning into me. Then it quickened its pace, sprinting down to the wall. When I finally caught up, it was snarling, "Off. Enough is enough."

Jerry grabbed the nearest thing, which was my elbow. The potto screamed, "Go ahead and make me," and the next instant found itself staring into the cheetah's bared teeth. "Oh," chittered the potto, "I wasn't thinking. I forgot that Cheetah bends." The potto tipped back, detaching all of itself but one foot. "I mean, thylacines by the tail are something else, don't you think?"

"Off," growled the cheetah. "Back to your cage. Everyone must be settled before the cleaning crew arrives."

The potto took my hand and released its last foothold on the cheetah.

"Wish my own cage," Jerry murmured wistfully as I rolled him and the potto under the wall and emptied out the platypuses.

The cheetah nodded to the waiting aardvark, slipped into the near distance, and vanished. Winifred and Ernest waved as I set off with the loris and the potto in my pockets and Benjamin still on my arm.

A moment later I heard two splashes; the platypuses were safe in their muddy pool. Soon, I told Benjamin softly, he too would be home and able to sink into the warm silent comfort of his cage.

We stopped at the Small Animal House so that I could drop off one furry ball. Everything was quiet there. The nocturnal small animals were just settling down for the day. The diurnal ones slept on. In the numbat cage across the aisle, the little auk stretched its short neck and ruffled its feathers. "There you are," he greeted us. "What a time you took." He waddled over to the rotten log, poked around in the crumbly wood, then shook a termite from his beak. He shuddered. "Some birds eat those things. I try, but. . . ." The sleeping numbat hissed a gentle snore but never stirred. "Now then," the little auk declared as it flew to my head, "there's one or two things to clear up. Did you think I'd forget?"

I stumbled out into the damp, still air, mumbling, "Too tired." Benjamin drowsed contentedly in the crook of my arm, but the little auk was as bright and sharp as morning. "How did you know where Thylacine would go?"

I was too tired to be cautious. "Dr. Hogg."

"You told her?"

I shook my head, which made him lurch and beat his little wings. "No. Not exactly. It doesn't matter now. She helped, whether she knew or not. She told me where to look. And why."

Benjamin murmured that if it had been him lost out there, he would have come straight back home.

"Thylacine didn't know how to. He probably didn't even know how he got where he was. Everything was strange and terrifying. After that bulb flashed—"

"That's the other thing," the little auk interrupted. "What happened to the picture?"

I managed a tired grin. "One thing that happened," I told him, drawing out a bent and creased photograph, "is lorises and platypuses." The photograph was so crumpled it was hard to make out anything in it at all.

We were at the Reptile House now. As I set Benjamin down in his cage, he peered over at the blurry picture. The little auk fluttered to the railing. "Didn't Dr. Hogg suspect? When you asked her?"

I thought a moment. "Not exactly. Only I had a feeling that in a way she understood, well, more than I said." I leaned against the clear smooth glass of Benjamin's cage. "But don't worry. She accepted my explanation, all right."

"What about that feeling then?" the little auk pressed.

"Oh, I don't know." I swung around. I'd had enough. I was too tired to figure out what I meant. I was just beginning to realize that some people really do speak and hear without words—like animals. "Maybe," I suggested, "I just imagined it."

The little auk sidestepped along the railing in front of Benjamin's cage, then flew the length of the Reptile House. "Imagined it," he repeated to himself. Just before he reached the door he hesitated, his wings beating hard to keep his chunky body aloft. "All I can say," he called back to me, "is that if you imagined it, there's probably something to it and we'd better all watch out."

16 I would have given anything to go to bed, or even to unroll my sleeping bag in Dr. Hogg's outer office behind the secretary's desk. But all I could think of was getting the furry ball out of my pocket and safely returned to the Observation Room before someone took a close look and found out it was gone.

You have no idea how hard it is to get into a building like the Institute outside of regular working hours, even if you have a key and it's perfectly legal. The thing is that at sunrise, when everything is dead still, you don't *feel* legal. And when you see the quite large back of a security guard turning the corner and disappearing into the milky-white mist, you can't help imagining him seeing you too.

I waited for a long time. When I thought no one was around, I dashed inside. I listened. I started up the stairs.

I was just going round to the second flight when I heard the front door open and shut again. So I ducked into the ladies' room. I heard slow, heavy steps pause, go on. I didn't dare come out. And there, sitting on the john, I fell asleep.

I woke up with a start. I heard a voice on the floor below. I heard the wheels of a cart rattling down the hall. As fast as I could, I ran the rest of the way to the Observation Room, opened the cage door, grabbed the furry ball still asleep in my pocket, and rolled it onto the cage floor.

When I shut the door of the cage, I saw myself looking even more smudged and bleary-eyed than that crazy mirror should have made me. So I ran back to the ladies' room to wash my face. I scrubbed and looked in the proper mirror and scrubbed some more. I was just beginning to realize that those weren't dirt marks but fatigue bruises, when Dr. Hogg walked in.

"Oh, it's you. I thought I heard someone in the Observation Room. What time is it?"

My heart pounded. I couldn't answer.

"How many more days of vacation?"

"Three." I wasn't able to count. "No, two."

"Not enough time." Dr. Hogg yawned. "This business with the tenrec . . . unforeseen . . . It's taken all my attention." She leaned over the sink and sloshed water on her face. Through the splashing she spoke about her reasons for inviting me. She muttered something about mixed motives. "Not," she added, straightening and reaching for a towel, "that I wasn't impressed with you."

I dug my fists into my vast, empty pockets. I looked

right into Dr. Hogg's face, still dripping and stuck with snarled hair come loose from the lopsided knot. For the first time the pencil was missing.

"I hoped we could become . . .hoped that eventually you'd tell me."

"But I did tell you. The thylacine. About sources, and all that. It was all made up."

Dr. Hogg's lips twitched as though she wanted to smile. "Yes, you told me that." She opened the door and beckoned to me. "You look as though you need a break. Get outdoors. Exercise and fresh air will be good for you."

Was she dismissing me? I felt all mixed up and miserable. I don't know why I said this, but I blurted, "There's a man in my school who's a bicycle freak."

"What kind?"

"Bike. He says it's his vice, exercise. What would you think of someone who bikes everywhere he goes and besides that does it just for fun early every morning?"

"I'd say he's probably very healthy."

"Do you ever bike?"

"Look," she said, "I've been up all night. I'm going to check the tenrec one last time because it's awake and still alive, and then I'm going home to sleep. Not on a bike," she added as she swung down the hall. "In a taxi."

Wordlessly I followed her, feeling ashamed that I'd forgotten to ask about the tenrec. Now it was too late to show interest. I just stood there watching while she stooped over it.

Suddenly, though I hadn't moved, she straightened up and raised a warning hand. "Keep your distance," she commanded.

I couldn't tell what made her say that. Keep my distance from the tenrec? From her?

I stepped back. She sounded so much like the cheetah that I was speechless. The cheetah couldn't stand us, Benjamin and me. It had put up with us as long as it had to. That was all. It would shun me now if I came to its cage. Though I never would. Not caged. Was that how Dr. Hogg felt about me? Then I was finished here too. I would never see her again, never wear the lab coat. I might as well cut my hair; it would never hold another pencil.

"If you intend to keep coming here," Dr. Hogg went on, "holidays and so on, that's one thing you'll have to learn. Like me. I'm always having to relearn about distance. About not tampering. Some of the pitfalls for people like us."

Did that mean she was letting me back? What did she mean, people like us? Was she an edge person too?

"About secrets," Dr. Hogg continued, placing the tenrec beside its water tube. "Like reminding myself not to corner you, even when I'd give anything . . ."

Our eyes met. Dr. Hogg gestured toward the tenrec. "If we can't keep this small biosystem functioning—"

"But it's alive."

"This time yes. But just barely."

I gazed at the bristly creature; it stood tottering on its bare, uncertain legs.

"There are some systems that are so . . .are in such delicate balance that simply by intruding we alter, upset . . ."

"Then what can you do?"

Dr. Hogg shrugged. "Keep trying. Looking." She

yawned again. "I could certainly use some helping hands."

I started to smile. Next time, I thought, I'd show Dr. Hogg how many helping hands you could get out of one inspired potto.

"That is," Dr. Hogg put in, "the right kind of hands. I need people with. . . ." She broke off.

I could feel my face grow warm. Maybe I'd been too eager; I'd misunderstood. Maybe this was a dismissal after all. "With what?" I babbled just to keep talking. "Sense?" I supplied, condemning myself for what I knew I lacked. "Honesty? Maturity?" What else was missing in me that justified Dr. Hogg sending me away to rest and fresh air? Looking down at myself, I was reminded of tumbling through the aardvark's tunnel and of the various animals I'd carried during the night. "Neatness?" It didn't matter about my knot falling apart; I wasn't going to need that pencil.

"I was going to say, staying power," Dr. Hogg said quietly.

I choked back the next fault. "You mean," I whispered, "like staying awake all night?"

Dr. Hogg shrugged off her wrinkled lab coat and held out her hand for my coat. I took it off, folding in the smears and pawprints.

Once we were in the hall, I could hear subdued voices coming from offices and labs. Someone started typing. A telephone rang.

"I've got to relearn how to keep some questions to

myself," Dr. Hogg said, as if suddenly recalling a lost train of thought. "Like how you managed to tamper with the one-way window." She rubbed her eyes. "Like how and when and under what circumstances you brought the potto back here. I suppose," she added shortly, "you returned the slow loris to the zoo?"

"But I didn't." Had I checked to see which furry ball I rolled into which cage? "Did I?"

Dr. Hogg was already down the hall. "Don't ask me," she retorted. "Don't ask what I can't answer, and I won't ask you."

"I . . . I didn't know," I stammered. "Honestly. It was . . . I . . ." So Jerry was in his own place again, home in the zoo. That meant the potto was here at the Institute with the one-way window turned right for him. Not only that, but Dr. Hogg would find him miraculously reformed and cooperative. His better self.

"There's a lot we both don't know," Dr. Hogg threw back. "And never will." She swung the door wide.

I was close enough behind to see what happened next. Dr. Hogg strode to the corner of the street, caught a glimpse of a cab just going by, and stepped out with all her commanding presence in view. The cab screeched to a halt. Dr. Hogg dashed for it, and at the same moment a man in a sweatshirt jogging in a loose sort of way came up against the great force of Dr. Hogg. He kind of crumpled. Dr. Hogg looked very angry. She raised him by the shoulder.

"You won't believe this," said the man, "but it's the second time within the last few hours that I've—"

"I believe," Dr. Hogg told him. "Get up."

The man got up.

"I have a taxi. If you're hurt, you may have it."

By then I was a part of the scene. I saw the man pull himself up to what I suppose was his full height, though next to Dr. Hogg it seemed to lack something. "I'm jogging."

"That doesn't excuse you from looking where you're going."

He opened his mouth. He gazed at Dr. Hogg. He mumbled something about a late night.

"I've had a late night. So has this girl. You want this taxi or not?"

". . . previous accident," he mumbled. "Sorry."

I said, "Dr. Hogg, this is Mr. Blanc. From school."

Dr. Hogg looked him up and down. "The bike . . . enthusiast? I hope you're safer on wheels."

"Usually I am," he said apologetically. "I had an unfortunate experience late last night. A large, savage dog attacked me."

Still looking at him, she said, "But not so savage as to leave a mark?"

"Well, I have means to protect myself. One has to with animals running loose all over the place. It's pretty rough when one of them jumps a person. Actually, there were two of them, but I only had to deal with one. Anyway, I'm all right. I suppose by now the dog is too. My bike's out of commission, though." He smiled into her grim face. "Nice meeting you. Even like this."

"Good luck," she said. "Easy on the dogs." And off she went in the taxi.

"Some people," he remarked, brushing off his elbow, "think more about animals than they do about people."

"She was up all night with a tenrec."

"With who?"

"An animal."

"Well, animals have their place, of course. But if you could have seen that mongrel—"

"It was a dingo," I said.

Mr. Blanc brushed his fingers through his hair. "Listen," he told me, "I'm off duty. I mean, this is my vacation as well as yours. If you need to speak to someone . . ." He looked around as though he expected to find just the right person to give me to. The street was full of traffic. The prompt people were already at work; the late ones were running, and the leisurely ones were taking their time. He looked into my blotchy face. "If you need me," he said, "I'm available. Any time. I'll give you my number." While he fumbled for something to write on, I gave him the pencil out of my hair. He picked up someone's parking ticket from behind a windshield wiper. He said, "Maybe we can talk again under more . . .easier . . ."

I nodded. It was too bad about Dr. Hogg. The circumstances of their meeting were not exactly promising. I heard myself say, "Sure. Another time." I watched him jog away down the street. I could tell he was heading for the park, maybe even the zoo.

Last night Mr. Blanc had seen a thylacine. What would he see today? Maybe if he went near the dingo's cage the dingo would recognize him and make some sign that would clear up Mr. Blanc's sight. I thought there might be something even he might glimpse of the invisible thread that tied us all together—Mr. Blanc and me and Thylacine and Dr. Hogg and Jerry and Benjamin and Winifred and Ernest and the little auk and the cheetah and even the numbat. I wanted to run after Mr. Blanc and drag him with me to see what surrounded him and held him.

At least, I thought, he had met Dr. Hogg. She had made her mark anyway.

But I had a vision of him jogging all alone, like Thylacine trotting along the empty gray streets and the crowded sidewalks and the dark, scary alleys.

I walked slowly home, carrying my decision to write all of this down. Because if another live thylacine shows up in Tasmania or here or anywhere else, maybe the Others will change their minds and trust some of us enough to bring their Beast out of hiding, so that he won't have to spend all his life alone and confused. I'm writing it for him, as well as for all my friends at the zoo and for Dr. Hogg who lives for them and for Mr. Blanc who is not alone, even if he doesn't yet know it. I realize it

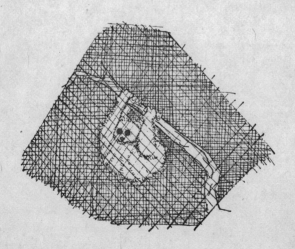

would be safe to show it to him any time, since he wouldn't believe it, but that would be playing another trick, and I'd like to avoid that kind of thing from now on if I possibly can.

Though I wish I could tell him, tell everyone, what Dr. Hogg understands about all we don't know and never will. Secrets are hard on edge people, especially those who tend to get carried away. If you consider how lucky we are to know as much as we do, isn't it still luckier that some of us are able to dream up what we don't?

THE NEW YORK TIMES

TUESDAY, SEPTEMBER 6, 1977

One of World's Rarest Animals Is Reported Sighted in Tasmania

Canberra, Australia (Agence France-Press—One of the world's reputedly rarest animals—a Tasmanian "tiger," or wolf—has been reported sighted in northwestern Tasmania.

Two policemen said they had seen the animal crossing a road while they were on patrol near the town of Derby. They said it had a rigid tail that did not move much as it ran, dark markings like rings on its tail, and small pointed ears.

Dr. Eric Guiler, of the zoology department of the University of Tasmania, said he believed the policemen had seen a Tasmanian tiger. He said he thought there were still some in the island state, which lies south of the southeastern trip of Australia.

The Tasmanian tiger is the largest of the known marsupial carnivores. There has been only unconfirmed evidence of its existence since the last captive of its species died in the 1930's.

These are REAL animals:

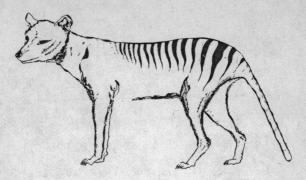

Tasmanian TIGER

Numbat

Tenrec

Tasmanian Devil